I0780539

Pudgy Knuckles

A Mibster's Story

LEAH LEE

ILLUMIFY
MEDIA.COM

Pudgy Knuckles

Copyright © 2024 by Leah Lee

All rights reserved. No part of this book may be reproduced in any form or by any means—whether electronic, digital, mechanical, or otherwise—without permission in writing from the publisher, except by a reviewer, who may quote brief passages in a review.

Pudgy Knuckles, a Mibster's Story is a fictional book based on real people, places, and events that I've experienced over the years. The main characters do not represent any individuals, but rather characteristics of many people I've known.

The views and opinions expressed in this book are those of the author and do not necessarily reflect the official policy or position of Illumify Media Global.

Published by
Illumify Media Global
www.IllumifyMedia.com
"Let's bring your book to life!"

Library of Congress Control Number: 2024921465

Paperback ISBN: 978-1-964251-25-7

Typeset by Jennifer Clark
Cover design by Debbie Lewis

Printed in the United States of America

CONTENTS

CHAPTER 1

MR. SEITLER

"Fourth grade!" Patrick exclaimed as he bumped elbows with his best friend, Curtis. They met on the cracked concrete porch at Patrick's house an hour before the first bell at school, each with a new pack of sugary bubble gum tucked conspicuously in their back pockets. A tradition they had shared since second grade was now the highlight of each first day of school. Shuffling their feet and occasionally kicking a rock off the road into some new hiding place, they stuffed the entire pack of gum into their cheeks allowing the juice to dribble out the corner of their mouths and off their chins. Curtis raised the back of his hand to swipe at it before it slipped down his neck. Puckered lips and puffs of air formed ever-growing delicate spheres and then pop! They would try again, each trying to outdo the other.

Patrick stared intently at Curtis's softball-sized, pink ball of a bubble. Suddenly, it collapsed as Curtis sucked the flattened wad into his mouth to make another attempt. "How many books do you think Mr. Seitler will hand out today? A heavy load maybe?" Patrick asked, his backpack feeling like a feather.

"Humph," Curtis managed to comment as the next bubble

touched the tip of his nose. "Beats me," he finally answered peeling the tiny bits of gum from his face. "Mr. Seitler doesn't like stuff like textbooks, you know."

Patrick maneuvered the lump of bubble gum into his right cheek with his tongue. "Yeah, that's why it's a good day to be in fourth grade." He looked forward to his first male teacher who everyone referred to as the Sky Guy because he kept a rather large telescope in his classroom, along with models of airplanes and Navy jets and handmade hot air balloons that previous students had designed and built.

"So Curtis, where do you want to stick our gum balls this year?" Patrick asked with a laugh because he knew that his prankish pal would place his hunk of gum in such a spot that an unsuspecting victim would end up wearing it home that day. "I know where I'm shoving mine. TJ Maloney gets his due today!" TJ, one of the class bullies in fourth grade, had been Patrick's nemesis for as long as he could remember. He and his cronies always called Patrick, one of the most obese kids in school, crude names.

Patrick was a blimp of a boy, overweight to say the least. His abnormally round face flushed rosy red every time he exerted himself, which also caused him to perspire profusely. Even slowly strolling the half mile to school left his armpits wet with sweat and his forehead lined with beads of salty water. He knew it was gross, yet it didn't matter because Curtis remained as loyal a friend as ever. And Mr. Seitler would certainly understand the nuances of being manly.

"There she is," Curtis said, pulling the pink slab from his mouth and curling his long, thin fingers around it to conceal his plan. "Gail, the gorgeous!" The two of them had a crush on Gail, the pretty blonde girl, for two years now. She sported a flowery skirt that bounced with each skip she took, and her frilly pink blouse seemed to catch every ray of sparkling morning sun, making her look like a beautiful spring blossom. The two boys gawked at her with tongues hanging out until the shrill bell rang.

"Hang on," Curtis said as he sprinted toward the swaying seats of the swing set. Patrick glanced at the classroom door as his peers began to line up against the brick wall while others moseyed toward what seemed the beginning of boredom. Then he noticed Curtis placing his wad of gum in the crack between the swing seat and the link loop on the chain. Somebody would certainly sit in that at first recess and spend the rest of the day with it stuck to their bottom. Patrick giggled. His prankster friend was as tall and thin as Patrick was chubby. Curtis had wild curly, fire orange hair and a ridiculous pattern of freckles that gave him the look of a spotted hyena.

Patrick and Curtis entered the classroom last while students searched for their nametags on the organized desks set about the room. "Please don't have me seated by TJ or Ben," Patrick muttered under his breath. Ben was TJ's bully buddy, the author of Patrick's third grade nickname, Fatsy Patsy.

Passing desk after desk, he caught sight of Gail on the far side of the classroom peering at the decorated walls of Mr. Seitler's room. He floated in her direction toward the empty desk next to her, at the end of the row. *It's gotta be my seat. They always put me at the end because I take up so much space,* he thought. He suddenly became aware of the elongated mass of gum tucked nicely beside his entire row of bottom teeth and even part way down his throat. Nearly gagging, he repositioned it until it lay crowded in his right cheek. Of course, it wasn't obvious because his face was a large lump itself.

"Here's your seat," Gail waved like a princess catching him in mid-breath. He could hardly suck in enough air to keep from passing out. *Yes,* he thought, *This is a good day to be in fourth grade.* Well, that feeling didn't last but a moment, until he noticed the edited nametag on his desk that read Pot Belly Pig. Hidden underneath was his real name, Patrick Melberry. Fake coughs echoed from the front of the room as TJ and Ben snickered and held back their absurd laughter.

"They're stupid!" Gail said as she ripped the added nametag and sent it whirling into the trash basket. "Hi, Patrick," she smiled, "How was your summer?"

"Uh," Patrick stammered as his mouth suddenly felt dry. "Good." The flush of warm blood filled his cheeks.

Mr. Seitler began a long, somewhat monotonous explanation about expectations and rules. Patrick took a half-hearted mental note while he sneakily slipped the wad of gum from his mouth and stuck it gently under his desktop. His eyes wandered, and his ears felt full of marshmallows as the droning continued. *How long does it take to tell about fourth grade?* he thought as he yawned. He glanced at Curtis who couldn't have shown more distaste for Mr. Seitler's sermon. Curtis leaned back in his chair and sprawled out like a limp noodle with his mouth open in a hollow expression. The other students wiggled and fidgeted for what seemed like an eternity and then, finally, Mr. Seitler suggested they all stand up and stretch. He apologized for all of the information he was required to present. Then he decided to engage them with a science experiment using eggs.

Patrick fumbled with the raw egg hoping he wouldn't drop it before the teacher explained the process of weighing, measuring, describing, and sketching their eggs "Ahhh!" screeched a girl in the third row. Everyone turned to see an egg splattered on the floor.

"I thought it was hard-boiled," said Curtis with a shrug of his shoulders.

Patrick smirked knowing that wouldn't be the only egg Curtis would send to its doom.

A little later, clear plastic cups adorned the windowsill. In each cup was a sunken white oval egg lying helplessly in a vinegar bath as tiny bubbles formed around its shell.

"PU, Pig Boy," TJ loudly whispered as he passed Patrick, "What did you do? You've stunk up the whole room."

Frustration built up like hot magma in Patrick's chest. He wanted to scream or smack him, but he restrained himself because he already had a plan. He just needed a little time alone in the classroom.

Surprisingly, the day didn't drag on with pre-tests, "get to know your classmates" games, or any challenging assignments. Instead, after Mr. Seitler guided them through the egg experiment, he started showing signs of the teacher Patrick hoped he'd be—laid back and off track. Everyone listened intently to the stories of his childhood; his wife and two sons; his three dogs, four cats, ten fish, and one slimy salamander. He was startled by the intercom call from the office informing them that it was their turn to line up for lunch.

"Okay gang," Mr. Seitler stated. "I volunteered to help move kids through the lunch line today, so let's show everyone we're the best behaved fourth graders ever!" He suggested they wash their hands on the way out, but only a few teacher-pleasers did so. Then, the entire group of twenty-four boys and girls followed Mr. Seitler like little ducks waddling their way to the feed pen. All that is except for Patrick, who stayed behind pretending to look for his sack lunch, which, of course, he never brought since he always ate hot lunches. What he really wanted to find was TJ's backpack.

Ha! Patrick thought as he swallowed hard. *That's his.* He quietly rejoiced and then fetched the just so slightly dried out ball of gum inside his desk. After stretching it like taffy for a brief moment, Patrick unzipped TJ's backpack and meticulously blanketed every tiny tooth of the zipper till it was a blah pink. Then he forced the zipper closed with way less effort than it would be to open it again once the gum solidified. "He deserves it," Patrick said.

By the time Patrick reached the hallway, the lunch line was still moving. No one had missed him. Despite Mr. Seitler's attempts to guide a handful of confused kids struggling to punch their forgotten lunch numbers into the keypad, it seemed as if a minor pandemonium might break out at any moment.

Patrick spotted Curtis scratching at a poster of a food pyramid taped to the wall. "We won't have time for recess, if they don't hurry up," Curtis said. "Did you do it?" he whispered.

"Yep!"

Curtis grinned. The lunch line moved forward a foot or two. They looked around at the full cafeteria and saw that TJ and Ben sat near the exit door, so they could be the first to the ball box. Patrick didn't care who got what playground equipment. In fact, he wasn't fond of recess. In the past, kids had laughed at him wedged in the slide or falling over the gaga pit wall because he couldn't climb over it. Ashamed of his size, he felt disregarded and unworthy of much of anything.

"TJ," the lunch monitor said within earshot of Patrick. "Your parents made it very clear to me that this year you're required to eat all your lunch before you head out to recess."

TJ groaned as his whole head appeared to have fallen from his neck in disappointment. He started whining about food and rules and recess until Mr. Seitler interrupted. "She's right, TJ," he said. "I was also sent a message to keep an eye on your eating this year since you threw most of your food into the garbage last year."

Curtis laughed. "Well, it's a good thing you don't have a problem with that, Patrick!"

Patrick nodded. He loved Curtis but even his best friend could add fire to an already burning flame. He did fill up his belly at every meal, however. To think that TJ was being forced to eat gave him such a sense of satisfaction, and he tucked that thought into his "as needed" memory box.

During recess, Patrick nearly melted under the broad shade of a tree. Curtis wandered off to check out the swing, wondering if stringy threads of gum would still be there. Patrick couldn't stand the heat of summer. All the other kids spent their time at the city pool, but he didn't even own a swimsuit. He wouldn't dare set himself up for the harassing he would receive by parading around in a beached whale suit, white as the moon, and bouncing like blubber. *No way*, he thought to himself. *Never!*

A group of girls squealed while flipping over and over a bar seeing who could get around it the most times. Gail played among them while Patrick stared. No girl could ever be as pretty as Gail with her sea-blue eyes, fair skin, and sun-yellow hair that flowed like a mermaid's. Her smile lit up the world, causing Patrick's heart to race uncontrollably. She challenged a couple of girls to the contest, and as she flipped, her flowery skirt blurred before them as it lifted and fell, lifted and fell. Patrick noticed the light blue exercise shorts beneath her skirt, and his entire body flushed with embarrassment.

"What's with you, Patrick?" Curtis said sitting down beside him. "You look like a tomato."

"It's hot!" Patrick panted from the heat as well as the blush that had turned his cheeks and arms bright red.

"There's hardly any gum left on the swing. I sure wish I could've seen it." Curtis giggled mischievously.

"I can't wait to see what TJ does when he tries to open his backpack at the end of the day." He used his shirt to wipe the sweat from his brow, giving Curtis a full view of his bulging belly.

"How many pencils do you think you could hide in the rolls of your stomach?" Curtis asked matter-of-factly. "I'm guessing at least twenty."

Patrick laughed. "How many pencils do you got?"

Ring! Ring! The recess bell blared. Patrick separated himself from the ground with great effort. Then he and Curtis wended their way toward Mr. Seitler, who stood smiling at the open door to the classroom.

"Class!" their teacher raised his voice. "Take turns getting water and try to save some for the rest!" Students kept pushing their way toward the sink, complaining that someone was taking too long. Mr. Seitler gave up and ambled his way to the whiteboard.

Although the air-conditioning kept the room cool and comfortable, the onslaught of hot, outdoor air mixed with the odor of vinegar and eggs created a gag-inducing stench. Everyone plugged their noses except for Curtis. Taking a deep breath, he raised his arms praising the day they all started fourth grade. Patrick laughed the loudest. His best friend was, well, simply the best.

Gail giggled sweetly. She never criticized anyone. She kept quiet unless asked to speak, except for when the bullies picked on people. Gail's heart shone golden in those moments when she took a stand against them. That's why he liked her so much. She was, well, simply nice.

The afternoon dragged on as the lessons blurred before Patrick's eyes. Social studies seemed sorely boring. Then Mr. Seitler asked everyone to write what a perfect day looked like. Patrick couldn't recall ever having a perfect day, so he created a ridiculous story about being crowned a king while his classmates bowed down to his authority as he raised his rod and scepter. Finally, after what seemed like a lifetime, Mr. Seitler handed out personalized folders packed with papers for parents to sign, and then he dismissed the bus riders first. TJ rode a bus to the rich kids' neighborhood.

Curtis shifted uncomfortably in his chair, pretending to gather supplies, but Patrick knew he only wanted a better view of TJ, who grabbed his red folder, tucked it between his elbow and waist, shoved Ben playfully, and turned to give a final glance at the cutest girl in class—Gail. Patrick felt like a steam engine knowing full well that she had no interest in bullies, yet feeling rather protective of her nonetheless. Then it happened.

"What the!" TJ shouted, sounding like a sick cat. "My zipper is —" he screeched. TJ yanked and shook his backpack as if that could magically open it. He appeared to have lost his composure and might actually cry.

At that, Mr. Seitler stepped closer to examine the evidence when the bell sounded, and the voice over the intercom gave the final call for all bus riders. Not wanting to disrupt the bus schedule, their teacher herded the handful of kids toward the door while attempting to unfasten the gummed-up zipper. TJ released his final explosion of frustration by threatening to end the life of the person who had done this to him. His wails could be heard down the hall.

Satisfaction filled Patrick to the brim. Curtis snickered. Gail seemed bewildered, and the rest of the class was oblivious to the commotion. Patrick never feared for his life even though the death threat had been directed toward him. TJ always threatened yet never followed through simply because he was a baby of a bully— all words and emotion but no evil action. That is, except for the dagger that dug deep into Patrick's heart, stealing his self-worth and leaving him feeling like nothing but a fat, pot belly pig of a boy.

CHAPTER 2

HOME FROM SCHOOL

"See ya later," Patrick hollered at Curtis, who strolled toward his house a couple of houses away.

Opening the door, the smell of baked cookies overpowered him. Deedee, Patrick's mother, skipped over to the entry to hug him tenderly.

"Pattycake, how was your first day of school? Do you like Mr. Seitler?" That nickname had stuck with him from babyhood. Deedee had sung the baker's man song to him repeatedly always emphasizing the word *Pattycake* until it stuck as a nickname.

"He's great!"

"Wonderful! Now, I'll take all those papers that I need to sign, and you just have a seat here at the table, rest your tired legs, and I'll bring you some warm chocolate chip cookies and some milk. How does that sound?"

"Great, Mom!"

"Here you are," she said, placing two cookies before him. "And your milk." Taking a seat next to him, she breathed deeply, obviously contemplating her next words. "Now, Pattycake, I want this year to be different from the rest. You'll be ten years old next month—a double digit child—which means you're ready to start growing up and taking life more seriously."

"Hmm," Patrick mumbled.

"I understand how hard it is to make new friends especially when, well, you know, when you're bigger than everyone else, and that's all they see. I mean, you're more than your size, and I love you. So, I think this is the year that you join an after-school activity. Maybe you can get involved in soccer or another sport. Maybe team running or even bicycling. Curtis rides a nice bike. Would you like one also?"

"I don't know." Patrick swallowed the last of his second cookie and downed the glass of milk.

"Maybe Curtis will join you even. I think it's a wonderful idea. Don't you, Pattycake? Life is difficult for young people. Soon you'll start growing into your body, but for now it would be helpful to get a head start. I'll encourage and support whatever you choose to do this year, so when the flyers start spreading around the school, keep an eye open for what you'd like to join." Deedee stopped. Her nervous behavior seemed to catch up with her spiel as she tapped her long, delicately painted fingernails on the table.

"What?" Patrick asked, dumbfounded. His mother often got lost between wanting him to lose weight and keeping him forever fat. What was she wanting this time, he wondered?

"Join an afterschool activity," Deedee said pointedly.

"Um, maybe. I guess I could." Patrick had no intention of joining anything at the moment. The thought of physical activity in a group setting where any of his peers could watch him fail miserably did not seem like a favorable way to start growing up and taking his life seriously. As far as he was concerned, he and Curtis would just continue their ordinary, prankster lives, getting even with bullies, watching cute girls, and doing their best to earn passing grades in school. Other than that, what else could life have to offer a two-ton cow?

"Oh, sweetheart, I'm so pleased that you're willing to cooperate. I have such fabulous plans for you, my adorable Pattycake," Deedee said as she took his round cheeks in her hands and kissed his sweaty forehead. "Your dad and I have a surprise for you this evening." Then she proceeded to clear the table and busy herself in the kitchen.

Patrick plopped into the plush recliner and within seconds, Fluffy, their fur ball kitty, clambered up the armrest and found a cozy place to curl up in his lap. She purred to her deepest content while Patrick pondered what his mom had suggested. He felt a glimpse of hope that perhaps he might actually one day slim down and play softball. He and his dad often tossed a ball back and forth, and although he tired easily, he enjoyed it tremendously. He imagined wearing the uniform with none of his blubber hanging out at the waist. He could almost feel baggy pants rather than pants so tight they bulged at the hips and knees, and maybe he'd fit into a jersey that revealed muscles instead of pudgy plumpness. Maybe one day.

"Meow," Fluffy stretched, licked her paw, then buried her little nose and whiskers into his belly.

"I could probably fit your whole head into the rolls of my stomach fat," he spoke quietly to her. Then he laughed at himself for ever considering a softball uniform. He understood why his mother hoped he'd grow into his body, because she lived her life for health and beauty. Deedee prided herself for being a member of the most elite gym in town, and if that wasn't enough, she sold make-up, and anti-aging products.

Deedee's friends admired her healthy eating habits and constantly asked for her special recipes. Strangely enough, she tended to cook separate meals for him and his dad who desired meals that included potatoes and gravy, bread, meat, and above all else, dessert. His mom shied away from sweets, yet always made certain a sugary treat was available. His dad called it a double standard, whatever that meant. She always insisted that Patrick clean his plate, but at the same time she complained that he'd gain weight if he ate too much.

Now, today, she wants me to join a sport, he thought. *I wonder if she'd be there to cheer me on or pull me out because she'd be worried I'll pass out or have a heart attack?* Patrick couldn't begin to understand his mom. *Oh well.*

"I love you, Mom!" Patrick shouted across the living room. "Thanks for the cookies."

"I love you, too, Pattycake!"

A while later, Patrick's dad, Chad, pushed open the front door.

Patrick woke from a drowsy spell and leaned around the head of the recliner. "Hey, Dad!" he said.

"Son, how was your first day of fourth grade?"

"Great!" he answered. "Mr. Seitler is fun."

Chad patted Fluffy and meandered into the kitchen to find Deedee. Patrick caught the familiar sound of smooching and covered his ears until it passed.

The lazy evening brought the family together in the living room to discuss Chad's difficulties with coworkers while Deedee listed her accomplishments for the day. Finally, Patrick felt as if he needed to add a little to the dialogue.

"What happens to eggs when you put them in vinegar?" he asked.

"That can't smell very pleasant," Deedee interjected.

"I don't know, Patrick. Why?" asked his dad.

"That's what we did in school today."

"Interesting," Chad replied.

"Well, then," his dad said, leaning forward and pulling a small box out from behind his back. "Your mom and I decided that it was time you owned one of these." He handed him a neatly wrapped item about the size of a package of bubble gum. Patrick ripped at the tape and opened the box revealing a Swiss army knife inside. A bit in shock, he briefly peeked at his parents, then duly flipped open every shiny tool. His mind flew to the heights of a soaring eagle as he pictured himself slicing away at branches to construct bows and arrows, prying his way into locked places, and building a tree fort with whatever tool was sticking out of the knife at the moment.

"Son, you are growing up."

"Don't take it to school," his mom said frowning slightly.

"I won't," he answered but figured it might make it into his backpack at some point.

"Let's try it out," Patrick's dad said as he motioned for Patrick to join him in his shop for the first time ever.

Patrick felt like he'd entered the Men's Club.

Stepping into his dad's shop, he first noticed the smell of sawdust with a slight odor of machine oil or something of the sort. "Dad?" he asked.

"Yes?"

"What do you do with all of this stuff?" Patrick asked, quite interested in the drills and saws.

"Aw! They're my prime tools for larger jobs like the bench I built last year. Do you remember that?" his dad asked.

"Oh yeah! It was cool," he said looking at his small knife in comparison to the heavy- duty tools. "Will you show me how to use them someday?"

"Sure, if you're interested, but not after first going through safety expectations. For now, we'll start with whittling and carving," his dad explained.

Patrick studied the different gadgets in his Swiss Army knife. He held the soft balsa wood in one fist and used the tiniest blade to scrape away a section of the block. Immediately, an idea came to his mind. "Dad, I'm going to carve a figure of our cat!"

His dad encouraged him to plan it out, but Patrick hurried with excitement till his carving looked more like a lizard with a misshapen head.

"Ugh!" Patrick whined. "I'm not very good."

His dad fumbled around in a drawer that appeared to be filled with old junk, and he pulled out an odd-shaped object. Handing it to Patrick, he said, "This was my first attempt at a horse when I was your age."

Patrick burst out laughing. "It looks like a dead frog!"

"That's what your mom thought when I showed it to her," his dad replied with a grin. "You learn as you grow, son. You'll create a masterpiece one day."

"When I'm older, like you," Patrick replied.

His dad patted Patrick's shoulder. "You can't become a man overnight."

The next day when the fourth graders stepped into the classroom, they felt trapped in a stinking torture chamber with no way of escape.

"Let's begin our day with egg science, shall we?" Mr. Seitler suggested.

Grumbling reached an all-time high as no one wanted to move an inch closer to the foul-smelling eggs bathed in bubbles of vinegar gas. They had swelled to twice their original size. No one that is except for Curtis. Lifting his cup of effervescent liquid, he passed it beneath his nostrils and quickly displayed a rather disgusted expression. He swirled it slightly, enough to move the egg around slowly in a circle. Then he did the unthinkable and reached his fingers into the moving mass, cupped his hand around the ballooned egg, and lifted it out like a frog out of water.

The entire class gasped while Mr. Seitler clapped his hands feverishly. "Well done, Curtis! Explain to the class what you've noticed."

"The eggshell dissolved when I first touched it, and now it has a soft and kind of rubbery skin," Curtis said as he passed the egg between his two hands. Surprisingly, the egg held together quite firmly even though it was transparent.

Other students crept closer, eventually handling their eggs in a similar fashion. Patrick was disgusted at the ball of white and yolk in his palm, and as he was dumping it back into the vinegar bath, shrieks filled the room. He looked up in time to see Curtis's egg hovering in mid-air for a split second before it dropped like a dead weight.

Splat! The impact sent pieces of egg in all directions, plastering the carpet, desks, and legs. Jumping out of the way, Curtis backed into TJ, who held his egg too lightly, so it ricocheted off a wall, leaving behind a slick layer of slime.

"You did that on purpose, you dummy!" TJ yelled at Curtis, who shrugged his shoulders.

"Enough boys!" Mr. Seitler exclaimed, trying to calm the commotion between them, but behind him a new war had begun between Ben and Patrick.

"You stuck gum in TJ's backpack. I know you did it, Pot Belly Pig Boy!" Ben hissed in a low voice so Mr. Seitler wouldn't hear him.

"Prove it, Barf Breath!" Patrick snapped back at him. Ben had thrown up all over the floor in second grade, giving Patrick a reason to create his own degrading nickname for him.

"I don't need to prove it, I know it!" said Ben.

"You don't know anything, Barf Bag," retorted Patrick, staring him down and making Ben take a step back.

"You're the worst person in the world and everyone hates you, Fatsy Patsy," Ben said while retreating yet holding his sharp glare.

"Stop it," Gail commanded. "You'll get in trouble."

Ben backed down.

Patrick beamed at her support.

"Students," Mr. Seitler said. "This is egg science, and these things happen. So let's not get riled up about it. Please place your eggs back in their cups, wipe your hands, and return to your seats. Write your observations and conclusions as to what you think happened to these eggs overnight. There're no right or wrong answers." Mr. Seitler didn't appear at all disturbed by the mess.

Patrick felt victorious this time, and Curtis got away with his stunt. And Mr. Seitler was the best teacher ever!

CHAPTER 3
MARBLES CLUB

Posters popped up on walls around the school, and each week Mr. Seitler handed out new flyers. Students buzzed discussing the best and most popular activities.

"Soccer? Nope. Team running? No way! Dance classes? That's not gonna happen." Patrick read a flyer describing free Frisbee lessons on the playground after school on Mondays and considered this one. A half sheet of paper fell from his grasp, and as he picked it up, he read, "Marbles Club for Fun and Competition. Huh? What's that?" Showing very little interest, he shoved all the advertisements into his backpack and yelled at Curtis to wait up.

"You're not thinking of joining something this year, are you?" Curtis asked.

"I told my parents that I'd think about it."

"You should just get a bike and ride around with me," Curtis suggested.

Patrick tried to picture himself peddling a bicycle, but all he could imagine was his rear end sagging off the seat and the tires going flat. "I don't think so." He thought for a moment and then said, "Hey, what about Frisbee? It doesn't cost anything."

"Hmm, when is it?" Curtis asked blandly.

"Mondays after school."

"Nope, that's my favorite show day. You know that!" Curtis exclaimed.

"Oh yeah."

The two friends kicked a stone between them for an entire block watching it bounce wildly off the sidewalk and into the street where they left it to its demise. Patrick was perspiring profusely by the time they arrived at his house. The air-conditioning brought immediate comfort, and he stood there a moment before dropping his backpack to the floor.

"Oh, Pattycake, you're home!" his mom said while hugging him sweetly. "Would you like a cookie?"

"Sure!"

"Celia's in your class. Her mom called me a few minutes ago and she's joining team running," she said with anticipation.

"Oh," Patrick said.

"Well, I thought we could look over the options this year. Do you have any flyers? We could talk about them if you'd like to. Or we could wait for your dad to get home and make it a family discussion." She paused. "Would you like another cookie, sweetheart?"

"Uh huh," he nodded.

Later, when Chad arrived, he kissed Deedee as usual and then entered the living room with a bag of items. He dug around until he found what he was looking for. "Son, this is between you and me. I remember when I was about your age and my dad sat me down for this discussion, and now I think you're ready."

Patrick had been relaxing on the sofa, but he sat up so swiftly that his head spun. *No, please no! Not that discussion,* he thought. He fixed his eyes on his dad's face with an expression of sheer fear.

"Ha, no, son, that will come later," his dad said seeing the panic in Patrick's face. He placed a plastic container into his son's palm.

"Uh, what's this?" Patrick asked.

"You don't know? You've seen me use this haven't you? It's antiperspirant."

"Huh?" Patrick asked.

"You take the cap off and rub it on your armpits like this."

"Yeah, I've seen you. What does it do?"

"It keeps you from sweating so much and takes away most of the smell," his dad said smiling.

"You want me to use it?"

"It's a man thing," his dad answered.

Patrick blushed proudly.

That evening, the Melberry family discussed after school activities. Sort of. Patrick's mom suggested soccer, listing all the health benefits it offered.

"Nah," said Patrick.

"Well, there's a city softball league," she said.

"Dad and I play catch, Mom," Patrick responded. "That's good enough."

His dad read the Frisbee flyer. "This looks good," he said.

"I thought so, too," Patrick said. "I'll try that."

That next Monday, Patrick wandered to the playground for Frisbee. The scorching sun shone down on the small group. Someone handed him a blue disc and expected him to send it spinning to another kid across the field. He watched the array of discs zipping through the sky, noticed a boy snatch it from the air behind his back, then flip it around with ease.

"Come on, pass it," an anxious boy yelled.

Patrick gripped the lip of the Frisbee, moved into position, and sent it flying fifteen feet before it lost energy and bounced off the ground.

"Well, go get it and try again," the boy shouted. "Don't just stand there!"

Patrick jogged heavily to the disc, felt the sweat pouring down his back, and bent over to pick it up. He held it tightly and tried again only to release it too soon, sending it hard into the ground and rolling away like a tire. Then, he turned around and went home.

Patrick's mom almost cried when she witnessed his disappointment. Then she proceeded to pamper him for the evening. Patrick had no other options. Activities just didn't suit him he decided.

A couple of weeks later, after class, Mr. Seitler asked Patrick to step up to his desk. He felt sure that his teacher had discovered the mastermind behind the bubble gum incident, so he started to fabricate a lie.

"Patrick, do you know what this is?" Mr. Seitler asked, holding out a glass sphere.

"Yeah, it's a marble," he replied.

"Yes, but what kind is it?"

"Uh, a shiny, round one?"

Mr. Seitler grinned. "This is called a cleary." He held it up to the light, so they could both observe the greenish transparency. "Now, what about this one?"

"I don't know," Patrick said frowning.

"These two different colored ribbons inside give it the look of an eyeball. This is called a 'cat's eye.'"

Patrick leaned in looking intensely at the twisted tints of color and smiled. "Oh, it's pretty!"

"Have a peek in my drawer," his teacher said. Mr. Seitler motioned for him to move around to his side of the desk. As the drawer opened Patrick saw a pile of variated marbles inside a plastic bowl.

"Wow!" He didn't know why he felt astonished at the sight. Maybe it was because they enticed him, or that his teacher allowed him the privilege of seeing the small collection. He just knew that he wanted to hold them.

"Marbles Club has already begun, but you can still join, Patrick. If you do, Mrs. Lee will hand you your very own set of marbles like these. I know her, and she's super nice. You'd like her."

"Um, I don't know how to play marbles."

"Most kids don't. It's an old game that's nearly died out. She'll teach you like she does everyone else," Mr. Seitler said emphatically. Recognizing Patrick's reluctance, he suggested, "I'll go with you next Monday. I haven't played in a while."

"Really? You know how to play?"

"Mrs. Lee taught me," Mr. Seitler said.

"Okay!"

Patrick couldn't wait to share the news with his parents.

When Patrick got home and told his dad about the marbles club, his father recalled that Grandpa Melberry used to shoot marbles as a kid before the age of television and video games. "He carried a bag of marbles on his belt loop to school every day," his dad said, reminiscing about the old stories.

"Pattycake, honey, I guess it could be considered a sport, but I can't imagine how you'd get any exercise in Marbles Club. I thought we agreed that you'd try a sport," his mother said.

"Sweetheart," said his father, "we agreed that he'd participate in an activity, and I think marbles sounds exciting." He patted Patrick's back. "Great choice, son!"

The following week, Patrick walked with the registration form in his chubby hand into the school gymnasium with Mr. Seitler at his side.

Mrs. Lee sat on the edge of a taped off circle on the floor with an open brown bin next to her. Students of varying ages tossed their backpacks against the wall and joined her around the circle. Mr. Seitler sat cross-legged with his little bowl of marbles in his lap, so Patrick dropped down next to him feeling somewhat nervous. Across the circle a young boy of about seven years old fidgeted excitedly while an even smaller girl next to him held her gaze on Mrs. Lee.

"Hi everyone!" Mrs. Lee said smiling. "We have a newcomer, so let's make him feel welcome. Leigh, please grab a bag of marbles for Patrick. Remember, hang onto your marbles while I'm speaking," she said.

Leigh, a middle-school guy by the look of him, handed Patrick a plastic bag of mixed-colored glass spheres. Then he crossed the circle and plopped down. Patrick rolled the marbles around inside the bag taking note of several clearies—the transparent type—one cat's eye, an array of shades of blue, and an interesting yellow and black one.

"Let's go over expectations and sportsmanship rules before we start today's game," Mrs. Lee said. She carried a sincere grin the entire time and acknowledged every kid present.

Mr. Seitler nodded as she spoke, so Patrick followed suit except that he didn't claim to understand all the sportsmanship guidelines. *I thought we were here to play marbles, not learn how to shake someone's hand,* he wondered as Mrs. Lee demonstrated a handshake.

"Look your opponent in the eye and say something encouraging like 'have fun,' 'do your best,' 'you're an awesome shooter, and I can't wait to play against you.'" Mrs. Lee continued to shake the girl's hand until she responded with a similar supportive word. "Don't make up something. Just say a truth. And remember, wishing them good luck is not what I want to hear. Marbles doesn't require luck; it demands practice and a good attitude."

Patrick stuck out his pudgy hand to practice shaking, and a boy from the fifth grade took it firmly and said, "I'm glad you're in Marbles Club, and I know you'll do well."

"Uh," he looked at the floor, the boy's shirt, anywhere but his eyes, and said, "Um, thanks." Pulling his sweaty hand back, he rubbed it on his own shirt, then took his place next to Mr. Seitler.

"We're playing a game called, Pickin' the Plums. So everyone, find a partner, and I'll show you how to play," Mrs. Lee said enthusiastically.

The game was simple. You line up fifteen marbles in front of you, and your opponent does the same thing about six feet away opposite you. The youngest player shoots first trying to "pick a plum," or a marble, off the opponent's line. Each one knocked off the line counts as a point. You play until someone has shot all the marbles off the other line.

Patrick and Mr. Seitler paired up. Mrs. Lee strode over, pulled the yellow and black marble from his bag, lifted Patrick's hand in hers, and exclaimed, "Oh, your shooter is called a bumble bee. See how it looks like one?" She had him make a fist, tucking his thumb into the crotch of his index finger. Then she placed the bumble bee on his thumbnail.

"When you flick your thumb outward, the shooter will fly out. Aim at a marble and remember to keep your hand pressed into the floor. Mr. Seitler will show you the correct body positioning. Have fun, Patrick!" Mrs. Lee left to encourage others in their games.

The bumble bee proceeded to slip off his thumb several times. *My fingers are too fat,* he thought. Yet, he carefully went through the motions to set it back in place.

Mr. Seitler crouched on his hands and knees like a toddler learning to crawl. "Like this, Patrick," he said.

"You look ridiculous!" Patrick said, laughing. Yet, he hunched over copying his teacher's example. "I'm younger, so I shoot first." Patrick figured that TJ and Ben would forever tease him if they saw how much of a pot belly pig he resembled at the moment. Wiping the idea from his mind, he concentrated on the opposite line of marbles and flicked his thumb with such power that the bumble bee zipped across the floor slamming into the marbles, causing three to scatter wildly.

"Wow!" Mr. Seitler shouted.

Mrs. Lee headed over at the sound. "Looks like you've got thumb muscles," she said, "You'll make a great mibster!"

"What's a mibster?" Patrick asked.

"A mib is a marble, and a mibster is someone who shoots marbles."

"Oh," Patrick said, pondering the compliment as well as the new vocabulary.

Mr. Seitler set up for a shot and knocked a marble off Patrick's line. He seemed satisfied.

The game continued until Mrs. Lee called time as club was over for the day. Between the two of them, six marbles sat spread apart on either of the lines.

"We didn't finish," Patrick whined. "We're not very good."

Mr. Seitler shook his head. "It's about playing the game, Patrick." He grabbed his hand, shook it warmly and told him what a powerful shooter he was.

CHAPTER 4
BAD HAIR DAY

Gail opened her rather thick free reader. She immediately became absorbed in the story.

"What're you reading?" Patrick asked as he pulled a tattered novel from his desk.

"What? Oh, sorry. It's called *Watership Down*, my favorite book." She looked at the page again.

Patrick contented himself with the fact that, although he talked to Gail minimally, at least he'd sat next to her since school started. Mr. Seitler explained that seating arrangements would change after the break. So, with Christmas vacation swiftly approaching, he developed the courage to express his liking for her. Nerves spun webs in his stomach and sent electric jolts through his neck and spine.

Patrick asked, "What's it about?"

"A warren of rabbits was gassed out of their burrows because a development company wanted the land. Some of them escaped, and they're trying to find a new place to live," she whispered.

Patrick felt at a loss for words. He desired to say something intelligent, but he muttered, "Um, who's your favorite rabbit?"

Gail dropped her gaze from the page and smiled so sweetly at Patrick that he gulped and felt the blood rush to his face.

"Pipkin. He's a baby bunny with white fur and a cute, pink nose," she said grinning as her blue eyes twinkled.

"Oh," he said, unable to speak, the words catching in his throat. So, he proceeded to stare at his upside-down novel while the words "Pipkin, a white baby bunny," hopped in circles around his brain.

After school, Curtis and Patrick strolled home kicking a golf ball-sized rock down the middle of the street. The stone stuck in a crevice, so they moved toward it.

"Did you tell Gail you like her?" Curtis asked.

"No! I couldn't."

"Just get her a gift. Girls love gifts," Curtis suggested impatiently. He stepped up to the crack where their rock rested in fresh, sticky, black goo. "Ah! This gives me an idea!"

"What? Give her a rock covered in goop?"

"No, not her," Curtis said mischievously. "Ben."

Neither had played a prank in months and Curtis seemed set on this one. He hunched down, grabbed a stick and prodded at the rock. "It's gluey."

Patrick dug at it with a pencil, but it remained unyielding. "What do you want to do to him?" Patrick asked. Ben lived only a block away from Curtis's home, which made escape easier, as they had discovered a year ago after dumping a bag of moldy, rotten carrots on his doorstep, ringing the bell, and running.

"You'll see," Curtis said. All of a sudden the stick dislodged the stone sending it and a trail of tar arcing into the air. He moved, but not fast enough. The entire glob of it plonked on his head, rolled over his ear, and down his arm.

"Ick!" Patrick squealed.

"Oh, dang!" Curtis yelled. "It doesn't wipe off," he said, scraping at his shirt.

"Your hair!" Patrick said, laughing. "It looks like a huge bird pooped on you!"

The boys hurried to Curtis's house, hoping his mom wasn't there. She reminded Patrick of a witch in disguise. Maybe they could wash his hair and shirt before she found out. Entering quietly, they snuck to the bathroom, poured too much shampoo on Curtis's head and scrubbed it over the bathtub leaving a mound of bubbles. They rinsed it thoroughly, but their efforts proved futile. His flaming orange hair carried the day's disaster into the kitchen where Curtis's mom stood, wide-mouthed and fuming. Immediately her eyes locked on Patrick.

"Patrick, what did you do!?" she screamed.

"Uh, *we* did it," he said sheepishly, eyeing Curtis who glared back at him. Obviously, he should have lied. "I better go now," Patrick said, crossing the room. He exited the house quickly and fearfully, wondering how his friend would look with a shaved head.

The next day, to Patrick's surprise, Curtis arrived much earlier than normal with backpack in hand, ready to walk to school—except that, his friend wore a turban of plastic wrap on his head.

"What?" Patrick said as he stared.

"I begged my mom not to shave my head, so she turned my hair into a peanut butter salad," Curtis complained. "She searched how to get road grease out of hair, and I'm not kidding you—she took the advice of every one of the sites! And the tar is still stuck in my hair! She said all these ingredients should break down the grease."

Patrick peered closer. He noticed a layer of odiferous oils beneath the tightly wrapped plastic plastered to his head. "What's in there?" he asked with amusement.

"You name it: mayonnaise, peanut butter, Vaseline, Italian dressing, and baby oil!" Curtis frowned. "She forced me to go to school this way to teach me a lesson."

"Really?" Patrick could hardly believe it, but before his eyes, the crazy concoction started oozing from beneath the wrap.

Ben rode by on his bicycle, did a double take and bellowed in laughter.

"I'm not going!" Curtis cried. "I'm ditching."

"Wait! My mom will leave soon, and I have an idea."

Patrick's mom departed for a shopping date with her friend just after Curtis and Patrick darted behind the garage. In her private bathroom, she had a shelf with make-up and hair products that she experimented with occasionally.

"Ah," Patrick exclaimed. "This color looks perfect. Curtis, get that gunk off your head!"

Curtis ripped the plastic wrap off his hair, poured loads of shampoo over the tangy-smelling mass and roughly massaged his scalp with his fingers. Rinse. Shampoo. Repeat.

"Hurry!" Patrick wailed. We'll be late for school!"

"Okay, it's mostly clean," Curtis said watching Patrick fumble with a tube of brown gel which he proceeded to mix with a white cream.

Like a whirlwind, Patrick applied the darkening mixture into Curtis's hair skipping the already black goopy part. "It says to keep it in for twenty minutes, but we can't, so I'll just hurry it up." Patrick snatched the hair dryer from the bottom shelf, turned it on high heat and aimed it at Curtis's head.

"Are you sure you know what you're doing?" Curtis asked. He felt strangely uncomfortable. His scalp burned. "Okay, that's enough! I'm washing the hair color out." He dunked his head under the running water till it ran clear.

Patrick threw him a towel, which he proceeded to wrap around his head, and within minutes they flew out the door on their way to school. The bathroom had seen better days, but at least they'd might make it to Mr. Seitler's room in time for the second bell. Patrick tried to keep up with Curtis. His sides ached, his head spun, and he knew he'd lose his breakfast in a matter of moments. He'd fallen behind and collapsed on the first bench he saw next to the kindergarten classroom. When he glanced up he saw quite a commotion.

Curtis's hair had gone through a frightening transformation. Ben pointed at him. "What are you? A tiger? A leopard? Or a freak alien?" By this time, a crowd had formed. TJ joined in the jeering. He leapt and bounced like a wild cat making ferocious fun of Curtis who crossed his arms over his rib cage. A strange smirk appeared on his face.

Patrick stared blankly as Curtis proudly made his way out of the group. He strutted with his chin up and shoulders back like he'd outdone himself. His hair had shifted from thick, curly, and orange, to frizzy with black streaks, reddish-orange spots, and a patch of bleachy yellow. On one side hung a lump of solidified, black, road tar.

Surprised at the sight of Curtis, Mr. Seitler pulled him aside with Patrick at his heels. "Would you like to borrow my cap?" he asked.

"Nope, I did this on purpose," Curtis replied quite confidently. With all eyes on him, he took his seat. He couldn't have been more pleased with the attention.

Patrick grinned impishly.

"Look, Patrick," Gail said handing him a small stack of photos. "I painted all of these ceramic rabbits to resemble the characters in my book. And see, this one is Pipkin."

In utter amazement of her artistic ability and also the fact that Gail's focus was on him, and leaning against him, Patrick melted in his seat. His heart fluttered too fast. He saw stars.

"There's only twelve rabbits right now, but I'm only part way through the book," Gail continued.

Patrick stopped breathing. Kerplunk! He hit the floor heavily.

Mr. Seitler shuffled across the room, reaching the sprawled-out student just as he came to. "Patrick? Are you alright?"

"Oh boy, am I!" he said, blushing and wearing a ridiculous ear-to-ear grin but feeling astonishingly comfortable in his strawberry-colored skin. Gail had actually touched him.

Gail seemed concerned but only for a moment. Then she put on her studious cap and paid attention to Mr. Seitler.

"Class, every year just before Christmas vacation, I offer an after-school activity. If you are interested, raise your hand. You've probably heard that previous students constructed hot air balloons and launched them into the sky." He handed out permission slips to kids with raised hands.

Still floating on clouds, Patrick's hand shot up before he even realized it. So did Curtis's. Not Ben's. *Thank goodness*, Patrick thought.

Somehow, Curtis's bad hair day turned out splendidly, and Patrick's thunderous crash to the floor paled in comparison to Gail's rabbit photos and gentle touch. However, when he returned home, his mother stood in the doorway, an extremely disappointed frown covering her face.

"Uh, oh," Patrick gulped.

"Whatever were you thinking, son?" she stammered, acting as if she might cry.

"Mom, I—I can explain." Patrick began with the tar and ended with hot air balloons, not leaving anything out. Shocked at himself for telling the truth, he hoped his parents wouldn't go hard on him. "So, can I?"

"Can you what?" his mother asked befuddled.

"Do the hot air balloons?"

Still with a look of shock on her face, she strode inside and disappeared into the filthy bathroom without saying a word.

CHAPTER 5
HOT AIR

"An obstacle course," Mrs. Lee finished her sentence.

Patrick stepped into the gymnasium feeling flustered at arriving late since he loved Marbles Club. Mrs. Lee motioned for him to take a place on the circle.

"As you see, the journey around the gym is loaded with challenges—some easy and some especially difficult." Her smile never ended. "Select any open obstacle and shoot till you hear the whistle. Then go find a new one. Keep track of your successes," she said.

Patrick couldn't believe Marbles for Fun Club was almost over. He had looked forward to it every Monday, always remembering to bring his old sock filled with shiny marbles. The original plastic bag tore the second week. He reached in and pulled out his favorite shooter, the bumble bee. That marble won him lots of games so far. He called it *lucky* even though Mrs. Lee reminded him that his skill had something to do with it. He wondered if that was true or not. She surely believed in him.

He'd learned so much about sportsmanship—shaking hands, saying thanks when complimented, giving encouragement, paying attention, and following the rules. He remembered to smile even when he wanted to complain or argue about certain shots. Above all, Mrs. Lee expected everyone to be honest. Patrick balked at first because he always wanted to win no matter what. Fairly certain that she never caught him cheating early in the semester, he often pretended to help his opponent with a shot, when in reality he sneakily moved his shooter closer to the mibs.

Patrick growled at himself now for wanting to cheat at the first obstacle; a cereal box with a ramp at one end and a paper towel roll attached to the other. The object was to send his shooter up the ramp, across the box and through the tunnel. He set the marble on his thumb, aimed, and shot. It zoomed right off the cereal box. He tried again, and this time his bumble bee disappeared through the paper towel roll.

"Yes!" Patrick cheered. The gym buzzed with exclamations as other kids beat their obstacles.

The next challenge seemed most definitely impossible. A tall plastic tube—probably an old bird feeder—stood on end with every hole taped except one which towered ten inches off the ground. A note by the obstacle read: "The goal: plunk your shooter into the air and through the hole."

"Hey, Leigh," Patrick called. "What does *plunk* mean?"

Leigh crouched by an obstacle next to Patrick trying to launch his marble over a two-foot-wide chasm. "Oh, it means to lean your hand way back, but keep your pinky knuckle on the floor. Aim and then flick hard. Hopefully, your shooter will make it through. Mine didn't," Leigh answered.

Leigh was the best player in the whole club. He hardly ever lost a game, and he most certainly did not cheat. So, Patrick concentrated on plunking over and over again, coming close a few times, but never making the hole. Congratulating himself for being honest, he moved on to another challenge. *What a fantastic last marbles club meeting*, Patrick thought.

"Hey, Patrick," Leigh said, strolling over. "Are you joining competitive marbles in January?"

"I don't think I'm good enough," Patrick said.

"No way! Remember, you couldn't even hold your shooter in your hand when you first started. Now, you're a pro!" Leigh clapped Patrick's shoulder. "Come on, I'm joining. Besides, Mrs. Lee has coached tons of beginners."

"Coached? Like marbles is a real sport?" Patrick could not believe it. He might actually have the opportunity to be like other kids. He could join a sport.

"Sure, why not?" Leigh said, snatching his backpack and tossing it over his shoulder.

"Uh, okay, yes, maybe," Patrick replied.

Later that evening, forgetting to talk to his parents about competitive marbles, he anxiously fumbled around in the bottom of his backpack. "I know I put it in here," Patrick whined.

"What are you looking for, Pattycake?" his mother asked.

Patrick definitely didn't desire to tell his mom about Gail and her photos of ceramic rabbits. She had given him a picture of little Pipkin for a keepsake. To Patrick, it might well have been an engagement ring. Unbelieving that he could ever lose it, he desperately dug deeper into the caverns of his backpack.

"May I help, sweetheart?" Deedee asked pulling the pack from Patrick's grasp.

"Oh, I guess," he answered feeling defeated. "It's a picture of a white bunny." As the days dwindled before Christmas vacation, he came to the conclusion that he must seal their 'relationship' with the perfect gift, just as Curtis suggested.

"Why, Pattycake, here it is. You must have tucked it inside this interior pocket," his mom said.

Patrick breathed a sigh and said, "What a relief!" He shifted his feet, staring at them for a long moment and then spoke up. "Mom, could we go to the gift shop on Main Street?" He prayed she wouldn't ask why.

"Why?" she asked.

Be honest, the hovering angel spoke over his left shoulder. *She'll get crazy concerned if she knows you love a girl*, the little devil whispered into his right ear. Back and forth they tried to persuade him.

Finally, he blurted out, "Mom, I can't tell you!"

His mom decided he intended to buy a Christmas present, and she assumed it was for her. She grinned shyly with that, "Oh, how sweet of you, Pattycake," look all over her face.

That evening, he stuffed the tiny, wrapped, gift box he got at the store into his pack.

The next morning, Patrick realized he had to give Gail his gift before he lost his nerve. "What if" scenarios clouded his thinking to the point he almost elected not to hand it to her. But when she sat down next to him and pulled out *Watership Down*, he flushed all of the what ifs down the drain.

"Patrick, do you want to know why this is my favorite book?" Gail asked.

"Uh," he stammered, wishing he could lift his hand from under the desk where he squeezed her gift.

"I see myself as a rabbit in their warren, and I pretend to have discussions with each of the rabbits. I can almost hear them talking to me. They all have different voices, especially Pipkin whose speech is soft and sweet, and sometimes it makes me cry," Gail explained as if she had written the book.

"Then, I hope you like this," Patrick said, trembling. He released the little box from his chubby fingers sliding it onto her desk. A few students giggled, but he floated high above them on a cloud watching Gail open his package.

"How did you know?" Gail exclaimed. "How did you know that Pipkin had a thorn in his foot?" She turned the bunny figurine over in her hand.

"I—I, he tried to speak. Of course, he had no clue.

Gail interrupted, "Look! Its foot has a pink mark on it, just like in the story." She proceeded to touch his clammy hand in sincere gratefulness.

The brush of her cool fingers across his wrist caught him off guard, and he feared he'd collapse again. Taking a deep breath, he managed to say, "So, you like it?"

"Oh, I *love* it!"

Patrick heard, "I love *you*." Whatever else happened that day, Patrick was oblivious to it.

"Hot air balloon time!" Curtis punched Patrick playfully as the end of day bell rang. "Let's go." The two boys, plus a handful of other students, accompanied Mr. Seitler to a workroom that no one but their teacher knew existed. Inside lay sheets of tissue paper, glue, and skinny strips of balsa wood.

"You may follow the directions given on this handout, or you're welcome to come up with your own design," Mr. Seitler said as he handed everyone a sheet of paper.

Obviously, Curtis and Patrick chose to create their own design. Everyone else followed the flowchart. The only suggestion Mr. Seitler offered the two of them was to use minimal glue and leave the opening large enough for a flame.

"That shouldn't be a problem," Curtis said sketching out a pattern on the tissue paper. "Cut these out, Patrick," he said.

Patrick dutifully did so. Their balloon seemed larger than the other students' so far. And as he added lines of glue to the tissue edges to connect them, he felt sure it was too much.

"No, it's good," Curtis said. He carefully raised their elongated balloon to inspect it.

"Everyone else used balsa wood for the frame of the opening hole," Patrick declared.

"That makes it too heavy to rise," Curtis said sneering.

Patrick wondered where Curtis learned how to make a hot air balloon. "Okay, whatever you say," Patrick agreed.

"Interesting, boys," said Mr. Seitler, examining their creation. We'll see how it flies tomorrow. "Hope for a cold day for better launching."

The next day, the weather didn't cooperate with Jack Frost. "How cold does it have to be?" Patrick asked Mr. Seitler.

"The temperature difference between the air and the heat inside the balloon must be significant enough to lift the balloons you all made," he replied. "We'll still attempt it," he said smiling.

Patrick envisioned his and Curtis's balloon filling with hot air and rising the highest since it was the largest. In fact, he'd daydreamed the whole day, paying little or no attention to his teacher or his lessons. He did pay attention to Gail, of course, glancing at her inconspicuously off and on most of the day.

Finally, launch time arrived. "Okay gang," said Mr. Seitler. "Let's gather the balloons and head to the north side of the building where there's less sunshine.

"Darn!" Curtis complained. "A corner of our balloon's tissue paper stuck to the counter, and now there's a little rip in it."

"Will that mess it up?" Patrick asked.

"Nah, it'll work."

"Uh, okay," Patrick said anxiously.

The other students laid their balloons on the concrete until their turn. Patrick noticed their quality compared to his and Curtis's. They resembled real balloons: round, evenly shaped, and with sizeable holes at the bottom. Theirs looked like an egg science experiment: lopsided, thin tissue in some places and thick in others, and way too much glue. Worse, the hole they made to let the heat in was half the size of the other balloons.

When Patrick pointed it out, Curtis said, "Don't worry about it. There'll be less space for the heat to leave once it's in the air."

Celia and her partner handled their delicate balloon with ease while Mr. Seitler lit the single-burner propane cooker. He directed them to hold the flap of tissue exposed on the top of their balloon until it began to lift. He carefully positioned the opening directly above the blue flames. Immediately, the balloon trapped the hot air and rose beautifully above their heads.

"Wee!" "Ah!" "Cool!" Everyone clapped enthusiastically.

The next one rose just as elegantly but climbed even higher. Then, Mr. Seitler called Curtis and Patrick over. They transferred their four-foot-tall balloon from the concrete to the propane burner.

Someone whispered, "It's too big, just like Patrick."

Patrick winced. "We don't have a tissue flap to hang onto, Curtis," Patrick said. "Now what?"

"Curtis, you're taller. Hold it up and pinch the tip of it between your fingers," Mr. Seitler said. "Patrick, hold it steady until I can adjust the flame for the opening of your balloon." Mr. Seitler reduced the heat, latched onto the rolled-up tissue rim and allowed a slight amount of hot air through the opening. It showed signs of filling up.

"It's working!" Curtis shouted. Indeed, the balloon gave the impression it would launch at any moment.

"You can let go of it now, Patrick," Mr. Seitler said. Distracted by the fullness of their balloon, Patrick did not hear his teacher.

Then disaster struck. Without warning, the extensive balloon became a fiery inferno. To make matters worse, the change in temperature created a gust of air launching the burning mass sideways instead of up. Everyone hit the concrete sidewalk as though they had been crashed into, head on by an ocean wave.

"Help!" screamed a girl.

"Run!"

"Oh, no!" yelled Celia. "There's burning pieces." She shrieked. Too late. The remaining balloons ignited and took flight haphazardly, sending ashes this way and that.

"My balloon!" shouted one boy, getting up from the mass of people that had fallen over after the initial inferno.

"What have you done?" shouted a girl.

"Calm down," cried Mr. Seitler, "Let's get the fires out. Grab some wet towels from the bucket."

Curtis was jumping up and down. Patrick didn't know if it was from excitement or distress. Students started flinging wet towels on all the burning balloons. It was a complete madhouse!

"Calm down, calm down!" Mr. Seitler comforted a crying girl and reassured all that the flames were smothered. "Sometimes these things happen, and it's a lesson we shall learn from."

Curtis burst into roaring laughter, bending over to hold his stomach. Patrick gaped.

CHAPTER 6

COMPETITIVE MARBLES CLUB

Christmas vacation had passed quickly. Returning to school meant more homework, but also, Competitive Marbles Club. He'd spent endless hours dreaming about it and could hardly wait until Monday, the first meeting. Patrick stood at the bathroom sink, sliding the soap between his hands, pulling his palms apart slowly while impressive bubbles appeared in the space. He thoroughly enjoyed creating foamy bubbles.

"Baby bubble boy!" TJ declared stepping out of a stall. "You can't just wash your hands like everyone else. You have to play in the soap, too!" TJ grunted. "You're such a pot belly pig. Oink, oink!"

Patrick flicked his hands, spraying the remaining froth toward TJ, who froze, not sure whether to cry or fight back. Instead, he turned on his heel and hurried down the hallway. At that, a memory surfaced. Patrick smiled saucily.

During morning recess, Patrick had faked illness, so after a brief interval in the bathroom, he hastened toward his classroom. TJ's backpack zipper crackled with the granular remains of the bubble gum still lodged in the minute crevices, yet Patrick searched for another item.

"Ha, see how you like this, bubble boy," Patrick muttered as he opened TJ's salami sandwich and scraped a slimy layer of soap off his palm and onto the bread. Replacing it the way he found it, he made his way to the nurse's office for a handful of crackers for his "upset" stomach.

Cattycorner across the room sat Gail, who was now next to Celia. Patrick gazed at Gail and then looked over at Curtis, who slumped in his seat in the front row. He himself had been transferred to the end of a row closest to the door. Then the intercom call sounded for lunchtime.

Curtis and Patrick nonchalantly walked together, both aware of the event soon to take place in the cafeteria. They sat as close to TJ as possible. Patrick normally devoured his food, however, today he nibbled at it waiting for the explosion.

"TJ! You're not allowed to throw this sandwich away!" the lunch monitor said.

"It's rotten!" TJ bellowed.

Ben nodded in agreement.

"Your parents don't give you spoiled food. Now, I know there're new basketballs in the bin, but that's no reason to excuse yourself early. Sit back down and finish your lunch!" she demanded.

"I will puke!" TJ said. As he took a bite saliva drooled from his lip, and he gagged. Then he forcibly spit it onto the table.

"TJ!" she reprimanded.

Curtis spewed milk from his nose splattering his lunch and Patrick's, too. Uncontrollably, he laughed himself into stitches and beat the table in delirium. Patrick could hardly believe his eyes at the gratification his friend took in the prank.

"*You* did it!" TJ hollered. He jumped up, pushed his way past the lunch monitor, and shoved the soapy salami sandwich into Curtis's hair and ear.

"TJ Maloney! Accompany me to the principal's office, now!" the monitor said.

Wiping TJ's lunch from his cheek, Curtis declared, "That was worth it!"

Patrick concurred.

Monday finally arrived. Mrs. Lee made quite a few small semicircles on the gym floor. In the center of each, she stuck a small piece of tape, and then a short distance from opposite sides of each circle she placed parallel strips of tape.

"Welcome to competitive marbles!" Mrs. Lee beamed. "We'll play Ringer this whole semester preparing for the state and national tournaments."

Patrick noticed Leigh and some other kids his age entering the gym, so he moved over to them.

"Hey!" Leigh said, "I'm glad you decided to join." Then, they all gathered around Mrs. Lee.

She passed out new plastic bags of marbles; this time every mib was dark blue. In fact, all the bags contained blue marbles and one new shooter, a marble slightly larger than the mibs. Patrick touched his and realized it felt a bit rough. Black and ugly, the new shooter didn't impress him. Maybe she made a mistake and gave him an old one.

Leigh reached into his pocket and pulled out a different shooter, one Patrick had not noticed before. Not shiny or even pretty, Leigh's shooter resembled a stone. He proceeded to roll it between his thumb and index finger in a circular motion with incredible control, then with palm up, he flicked it sending it speeding to the floor. It spun! And remained in one spot.

"How did you do that?" Patrick asked astonished.

"It's called backspin," Leigh replied. "Mrs. Lee will show you."

He couldn't wait. Patrick pinched his new shooter, copying Leigh's actions, and flicked the marble halfway across the gymnasium. He cowered, expecting to be scolded for not hanging onto his marbles.

"Wow!" A girl squealed.

"Power!" Leigh said.

"When you learn to control your backspin and aim, with that kind of power, you'll be a force to be reckoned with, Patrick," said Mrs. Lee. "Now, go get it and wait for directions."

She showed everyone how to play Ringer. A very old game, apparently almost forgotten, Ringer used to take place outside on the ground where opponents traced circles—a pitch line, and a taw line—with their fingers in the dirt. Mrs. Lee threw out such a new string of marble vocabulary that Patrick imagined they'd be quizzed, and he panicked.

"Relax. You'll learn them," Leigh whispered. "I'll be your opponent today," he said.

Mrs. Lee continued. "We'll work on different skills each week, perfecting them as we go. Don't worry if you struggle, that's part of learning." She smiled seriously. "Above all else, I expect superb sportsmanship."

Then, from her brown bin she extracted what looked like weapons, strange devices that she called racks were strips of wood formed in the shape of a cross with little holes drilled through them equal distances apart. "Thirteen holes, thirteen marbles," she said. Demonstrating how to create the *rack* inside the circle, she used her toes to press on two ends of the wooden rack, then lifting it carefully, thirteen perfectly aligned marbles remained in the center of the circle.

"Whoa!" Patrick's mind spun, his hands shook, and his fingers fumbled with his new shooter. He wanted his bumble bee. "What's with this shooter?" he asked.

Leigh responded, "The rougher the shooter, the easier it sticks inside the ring. Yours is glass, and it seems like Mrs. Lee sanded it some."

"What's your shooter, then?"

"Mine is an aggie, a marble made of agate stone. Look closely. See the layer upon layer of rock that it was cut from?" Leigh said.

Patrick touched it, and although the aggie felt rough, he recognized tiny seams of varied colors of stone that made up his dull, tan-colored shooter. "Where did you get?"

"If you make the team, Mrs. Lee will fit you for your own agate," Leigh said.

Cold sweat broke out all over Patrick's skin as he considered *not* making the team. He hadn't realized the pressure he now faced, and he feared the worst. During the rest of the club, Leigh pounded him and drug him through the mud every single game. Patrick had been obliterated, and although he should've left the gym that day drooping like a wet dog, he felt invigorated and inspired by Leigh's ability.

I'm going to learn how to shoot like him, Patrick thought as he shook Leigh's hand and told him what an awesome player he was.

Leigh replied, "Keep practicing and you're going to do great!" He gave Patrick a firm handshake.

Practice. Yes, that seemed to be the key to this sport, he decided. When Patrick arrived at his house, he tossed his backpack on the floor, pulled the new bag of marbles from his pocket, and fingered the ugly black shooter. He tried to place it correctly on his thumb as he had observed Leigh doing, but he hadn't learned backspin yet —Mrs. Lee promised that for week two. Then he attempted to place the mibs three inches apart in the shape of a cross on his bedroom carpet.

"Darn it!" The marbles wouldn't stay in place. The carpet had little bumps. When he aimed, his shooter shimmied, and to make things more frustrating, the mibs he knocked out of the makeshift circle rolled behind his dresser, under the bed and even beneath his door. By the time he finished one game against himself, he had lost two of his new blue marbles.

"Dad," Patrick complained, "I need some extra marbles to practice with. I've already lost my marbles," he whined.

His dad laughed. "You've lost your marbles!"

"Well, not all of them. What's so funny?" Patrick asked, quite perturbed at his dad.

"'You've lost your marbles' is an old saying that means you've gone crazy." His dad said. "I haven't heard that term used in a long time." He realized Patrick's discontent, so he agreed to purchase some and asked Patrick to ask his teacher where to get the marbles.

The following week, Patrick approached Mrs. Lee and inquired, "Where did you buy all these marbles?"

"They've been donated, thousands of them, actually. A woman in another city heard about our club and offered them to me as a gift."

"Oh, wow!" Patrick sighed. "I want to buy some more, but I want to make sure they are quality ones."

"I understand. Did you know that only one marble manufacturing company exists in the United States as of today?" she asked. "It's called Marble King. I know the CEO, and she is part of the National Marbles Tournament board and a sponsor of the tournament. So you can imagine what fantastic marbles we use there."

"You know her?" Patrick glowed. "Can I buy some from Marble King?"

"Yes, they mostly make them in bulk, but I imagine you'd like a smaller batch?"

"Yeah, I guess," Patrick said.

"I'll see what I can do," Mrs. Lee said.

"Gosh, thanks!"

Patrick couldn't wait to learn backspin. However, his shooter sat awkwardly in his fingers. He assumed they were far too fat for this position. Mrs. Lee had used a marker to draw lines on the outside of his right thumb knuckle and the inside of his index finger. He made an effort to keep the marble stuck there so he could lay the back of his hand on the floor, straighten his wrist, and prevent his knuckles from leaving the ground when he flicked his thumb out.

"What?" Patrick frowned. "I flicked, and it fell in my hand. It didn't even go anywhere!"

A girl crouching on her hands and knees next to him shot her marble so crookedly that it hit Patrick's wrist. "Keep trying. We'll get it!" she said.

Discouraged after several attempts, he called for help. "I can't do this."

"When you say you can't, then you *can't,*" Mrs. Lee replied. She kneeled beside him, stuffed his shooter into position, and told him to squeeze it in place until it hurt.

"Ow, there's a dent in my thumb," Patrick cried.

"Exactly! It's the beginning of the coolest callous every mibster develops over time. Now, do it again."

"Ow!" he squeezed it harder.

"Are you ready to practice backspin, Patrick?" asked Mrs. Lee.

He allowed her to hold his wrist to the floor as she guided him through the movement of his index finger and thumb, so his shooter rolled from his knuckle to fingernail. She had him practice that roll until he could control it. Then Mrs. Lee told him to give his shooter a little flick.

"It's spinning! Instead of rolling away, it's staying in the same spot!" Patrick yelled excitedly. He glanced at Leigh who nodded encouragingly.

CHAPTER 7
MR. JERRY

Halfway through competitive marbles semester, a guest speaker showed up in the gymnasium. Leigh was absent that day, so Patrick chose to sit with some boys from middle school. They included him in their small group and treated him as a friend. In fact, nearly all of the kids in Marbles Club were kind to him. Even better, no one teased him about his unusual size. Nonetheless, he hadn't come to terms with himself and still felt like Fatsy Patsy and Pot Belly Pig Boy, a worthless part of humanity.

Mrs. Lee introduced their guest as her father, Mr. Jerry. An older man, he seemed enthusiastic and carried a mysterious gun case with him. He advised everyone to scoot in so they could see.

"I've come for three reasons," he said. "One, to tell stories. Two, to enlighten you. Three, to offer you an invitation." He began. "When I was a young boy, I attended a one-room schoolhouse, and all the students sat in straight rows according to their grade. We all had one teacher, so when she was busy with one row of kids, everyone else had better be quiet and work hard."

A girl raised her hand. "Mr. Jerry, my great grandpa told me that his teacher smacked him with a ruler back then. Did you ever get smacked?"

"Aw, yes," he answered. "Teachers required discipline, and a whack with a ruler or switch was common."

"During recess," he continued, "since no playground equipment existed, not even a swing set, the boys often shot marbles, and the girls played jacks or jumped rope." Mr. Jerry grinned. "I shot quite well, in fact. We used to play for keeps, which means that if you hit someone else's marble with your shooter then you got to keep it. Needless to say, I acquired a lot of marbles."

Someone else raised their hand. "How many did you have?"

"I don't remember how many back then, but right now I've collected over a quarter million."

Gasps arose. Mrs. Lee suggested they save their questions for the end.

"I had a favorite glass shooter, a three-quarters-inch one that was pale green with a pale white patch on it. And I carried my marbles in a leather bag tied with a string. If the teacher heard a marble fall on the floor, she'd take it. One day, I really wanted to look at some marbles I'd won at recess, so I carefully opened my bag to peek in, and the next thing I knew some of the marbles spilled onto the hardwood floor, making a loud racket."

"Oh, no!" Patrick cried.

Mr. Jerry nodded. "She gathered up every single marble as I sat shaking at my desk. She proceeded to unlock a tall file cabinet and dump my marbles into a jar. When she re-locked the cabinet, I was left with a void in my heart." He sighed. "Marbles meant something special to kids during my time, and mine were my favorite possessions. I counted and sorted them often. My brothers and I spent a good deal of time playing games and trading with each other, but that day at school broke my heart. Not only had I lost a good portion of them, but my favorite shooter lay in a dark abyss."

Patrick's heart was pounding with anticipation.

"Finally, on the last day of school, our teacher marched to her filing cabinet and withdrew a full jar of marbles that she'd collected throughout the year. She left us inside while she went out to the playground. When she entered again, she said, 'I've hidden all of them. Whatever you find, you may keep.' Then she released us. I thrust my way to the front of the line and rushed outside for the hunt."

"Did you get them all back?" a young boy shouted. "Did you?"

"When I realized how quickly people found handfuls of them, I decided to focus on locating my shooter before someone else got ahold of it." Mr. Jerry paused. "I was too late! A girl proudly showed off my marble to her friends."

"No," Patrick wailed. He felt as if someone had stolen *his* bumble bee.

"I begged her for it. I offered to pay her a quarter for it—believe me, that was a lot of money back then." She told me no. So I asked her if there was anything I could do to get it back. She contemplated for a while and then answered, 'Yes.' "

Sighing, Mr. Jerry continued. "She told me I'd have to come over and play house with her," he said, shaking his head. "'Was my shooter really worth it' I wondered. That weekend, I sat at her tea party table wearing an apron and acting like a little girl. In the end, she handed me my shooter. And the worst part," Mr. Jerry said, "I ended up losing that marble sometime later."

Patrick felt like a heavy ball had fallen from the sky and landed on his stomach. "You lost it?" he asked.

"I've collected many other marbles though," said Mr. Jerry.

He opened the gun case and turned it so the contents were visible. One by one, he displayed the most incredible marbles Patrick had ever seen. He even passed them around so the kids could examine and touch them. They looked nothing like the glass mibs he'd played with. In fact, some were not even glass at all. Instead, clay, rock, and gemstone spheres dotted the foam-filled trays inside the gun case. Each was labeled with its title and worth.

"This one," Mr. Jerry spoke precisely, "May be the oldest

marble ever discovered in the ruins of a Chinese archeological site. Definitely handmade with rare white clay, it was meticulously molded into a near perfect sphere with intricate red lines painted around it."

Patrick hadn't considered the fact that some marbles were handmade, making them rare and worth more. He fondled the glass onion skin, imagining the myriad colors inside of it. A boy passed him a sulfide, a marble with miniature air bubbles, but more important, a tiny rabbit figurine peered at him from the center of the ball of glass.

Patrick grinned and thought, *Gail would like this.*

"Even the first machine-made marbles carried their own unique flavor. Slags," Mr. Jerry said, holding up a marble, "received names based on their color or markings like a number nine slag, a root beer, or cobalt."

Mr. Jerry explained that collecting marbles was one of his pastimes as was holding the Colorado Invitational Marbles Tournament every summer. "I'm here to invite any of you who are interested to participate." He encouraged them to sign up and keep practicing.

After club, while moseying home, Patrick thought about the remarkable marbles, and he determined to start his own collection.

That evening, Patrick laid his small set of mibs and shooters out on his floor, examined them closely, and sorted them into differing hues. After thinking about it for a bit, he went to his parents and asked, "May I participate in the Colorado Invitational Marbles Tournament?" He paused and then said, "And—and I need a gun case."

His mother jumped up in a panic. "Pattycake, have you and Curtis been experimenting with guns? I know his dad hunts, and I've seen some of those weapons. Oh my! Has he allowed you to use them? Whatever can we do, Chad?" She breathed too fast and held her chest as if she might have a heart attack.

Chad replied calmly, "Tell us more about this tournament and gun case." He surveyed his wife and said, "And honey, sit down!"

After Patrick described Mr. Jerry's visit and explained how he kept his marbles in a gun case, his mother's fears were resolved and he'd received permission to attend the tournament. However, his mother insisted he keep his collection in a lockable briefcase instead.

Mr. Seitler's class gathered around a rather immense papier-mâché' volcano that they'd constructed. The mountain was two feet tall and three feet in diameter and was painted brown and green and decorated with craft trees. It rested on a sheet of plywood on the playground. A quart of crimson-colored vinegar sat positioned nearby.

"We've studied the inner workings of magma, lava tubes, and eruptions this year," Mr. Seitler said. He placed a cup of dry ice on the opening of the volcano where it "smoked" for a short while. Removing the cup, he swiftly poured the vinegar down a funnel and through a rubber tubing into the belly of the mountain.

Curtis leaned in for a closer look when without warning the volcano exploded spewing "molten lava" sky high.

"Awesome!" he shouted raising his hands palms up to capture as much of the rapidly descending concoction as possible. Patrick crowded in to join him. Everyone else screeched and retreated. Mr. Seitler had once again wowed the students with another crazy mess—an educational one, of course.

"In order for you to understand this event, each of you will reproduce this physical transformation by mixing vinegar and baking soda together." He explained the science behind it and then handed each student a plastic water bottle containing a small amount of baking soda. In addition, they received a tiny cup of vinegar.

"When I countdown to zero, pour the vinegar into the bottle, hold your hand over the opening, shake it up, and release."

Curtis's eyes lit up with anticipation. Patrick caught on quickly as if he'd read his friend's mind.

"...three, two, one, zero!"

Pandemonium broke out. Some kids let go of their bottles which sped away spinning in all directions and spraying lava everywhere. Others removed their hands from the bottle tops, causing a shower of vinegar overhead. But Curtis and Patrick took expeditious aim, found their targets, and whoosh! TJ and Ben took the impact to the head and shoulders. In the frenzy of the moment, they stood dazed and confused.

"Holy moly," Patrick howled. Vinegar soda leaked from his ear.

"Whoa!" Curtis exclaimed absolutely reveling in the chaos.

Mr. Seitler called out to his class with arms waving wildly. "My mistake, my mistake!"

Dumbfounded and dripping, the students stood motionless as their teacher surveyed the predicament.

"I believe I should've directed you to hold your bottles and aim in the opposite direction from yourself and others." He surveyed the mess and then dolefully said, "Don't worry; it washes off, gang."

Summer vacation seemed to arrive too soon. Mr. Seitler, stood at the exit saying goodbye to each student as they left the building. Some cried, some held back to hug their teacher, but a grinning Patrick reached out and took Mr. Seitler's hand and said, "Thank you for the best year ever!" If there was one thing he'd learned from Marbles Club, it was sportsmanship—gratefulness expressed with a handshake and a smile.

CHAPTER 8
YARD SALE

"Mrs. Lee invited us to work a fundraiser the weekend before the tournament," Patrick said. "It's a huge yard sale at Mr. Jerry's house in Gunnison."

His mother hemmed and hawed. Her summer plans always seemed to take precedence, and this didn't fit into them.

Patrick looked to his dad.

"Son, if you'd really like to help, I'll take you for the day," his dad said, realizing that Deedee had just placed her hands on her hips and scowled.

"Can Curtis come, too?"

"I suppose so," his dad answered.

The yard sale, an annual fundraiser for competitive marbles, brought in a vast amount of money, but it required a great deal of workers. People had donated some expensive items, such as a truck and a boat, to support the age-old game of marbles. Kids like Leigh who qualified for the national tournament were expected to help, but Patrick felt compelled to do his share.

Only a week after school ended for the year, Mrs. Lee held an official qualifying tournament for kids interested in competing nationally. A handful of students played in this tournament, shooting on fourteen-foot by fourteen-foot concrete pads painted with ten-foot diameter, yellow circles. Sand had been mixed with the paint to simulate the pads on the beach at Ringer Stadium in Wildwood, New Jersey, where the national tournament was held. The three concrete rings sat on a raised piece of ground in the city park. When Patrick saw the official rings and strict rules he became anxious, so he watched but refused to participate, believing he had no chance of qualifying.

"Practice a lot!" Leigh had told him. "You don't improve by not playing."

Patrick had struggled with spending even half an hour a day of flicking, aiming, and shooting. Feeling fat and lazy dragged him down, and he disliked practicing alone. He spent a fair amount of time gathering and collecting new and old marbles, and since he loved the games, he wanted to support Leigh, Mr. Jerry, and Mrs. Lee.

So, the day of the yard sale Chad and the boys awoke in the dark to make the two-and-a-half-hour trip by 6:00 a.m. Arriving at Mr. Jerry's place, they spied him removing tarps from the tables. Early morning dew slipped down the sides of the tied down tarps. The crisp air bit into Patrick's bare skin.

"It's cold! I thought summer was supposed to be warm," he said, shivering.

Mr. Jerry laughed. "This is Gunnison, Colorado, one of the coldest places in the United States."

"Oh."

"Hey Patrick," Curtis called out. "Help me pull this tarp off." He wrestled with the enormous plastic sheet that protected four ten-foot tables covered in items for sale.

Taking in the site, Patrick was shocked by the immensity of the yard as well as the quantity of goods laid out. He grabbed hold of a corner of the tarp, and together they furled it and shoved it under a table with empty boxes. Mr. Jerry asked them to uncover the rest of the twenty tables scattered about the yard.

"So much stuff!" Curtis exclaimed. "There's no way it's all going to sell."

"Oh, don't be surprised, Curtis," Mrs. Lee, who was working nearby, sweetly corrected him. "More than half will go today and nearly all the rest tomorrow. And boys, your job is to see to it that it happens. Make yourselves familiar with *and where* every item is so that you can lead people to what they're looking for."

Before the sun rose, shoppers wound their way between the tables like ants gathering food. People snatched this tool, that toy, those clothes quicker than Chad, who had offered to run the cash box and sales, could keep up with purchases. When a long line formed, Mrs. Lee took up a second cash box. She had been refolding clothes that customers carelessly tossed while digging for the perfect outfit.

Curtis scurried while Patrick plodded for what seemed like hours as the sun beat down.

"It's hot!" Patrick complained.

"Make up your mind," Curtis said. He fiddled with a bird cage, tapping the swing inside.

"Maybe Mr. Jerry will let us take a break," Patrick said.

The boys crossed over to the purchase table where Patrick's dad busily sold one item after another. A customer bargained for a cheaper price on a space heater while Mr. Jerry considered it. A handshake later, the guy carried the heater to Chad.

"Mr. Jerry, could we take a break?" Patrick asked, panting while standing under a tree, trying to find some relief in what little shade it provided.

"You've been working this whole time?" Mr. Jerry asked, surprised. "Of course! There's snacks and sodas in the old garage over there."

Leigh stumbled out of the dank-smelling building with an iced soda in his hand. "How's it going, Patrick?"

"It's hot," he replied.

"True," Leigh agreed. "This place is rustic. You'll see."

Closing the door behind him left them in shadowy darkness. He felt around for the cooler and Patrick dipped his arms up to his elbows into ice water and soft drinks. Cupping as much freezing water into his hands as he could, he showered Curtis who threw his head back in delight. They popped open two refreshments and gobbled down an entire package of cookies. The place was packed with rusty tools, splintered wooden boxes, antique items that neither could identify, and a beat-up pick-up truck. Blotches of oil and grease lay here and there. Peering up into the dim, dusty garage, they could almost make out a second level.

"Are there steps? Or a ladder?" Patrick asked.

Curtis tried to find a light switch to no avail. He scooted around sending dirt and dust bunnies rising into the musty air inside. A sliver of light shown through cracks in the walls, highlighting hanging spider webs.

"Creepy," Patrick uttered.

"A rope!" Curtis shouted holding the pokey coil in his fist.

Hastily, they tossed a knotted end up and over a rickety two-by-six plank. It arced over and bounced off the floor sending dust into the air. Curtis yanked on the rope securing one end of it to a vice attached to a worktable. He latched on and began to clamber up the rope. Patrick attempted to hold it steady. Small chunks of rotten wood rained down on him.

Grunting, Curtis reached a set of planks and called down to Patrick, who rubbed his eyes. "Hey," Curtis blurted out. "It's a loft of some kind that leads to a square door."

Blinded by the falling wood particles, Patrick encouraged him to investigate. "Hold onto the rope just in case." He opened his eyes a sliver to see his friend crawl away into blackness.

Suddenly, there was an explosion of light and fractured wood, and the highest pitched howl that Patrick ever heard blasted his eardrums. Dust enveloped the garage as Patrick stumbled around trying to escape the mayhem. Outside, at the other end of the building, Curtis dangled from a second-story window with one fist wrapped tightly around the rope and the other flailing around for anything solid to grab ahold of.

"Help!" Curtis cried. "Help!"

Patrick coughed. Eyes watering, he saw a mirage of people rushing to Curtis's rescue. He moved to follow them creeping like a crippled tortoise. His legs felt like noodles, and his heart raced with dread. Like a dream where one can't budge, he was suffocating from fear.

Leigh grabbed ahold of Patrick and dragged him into the commotion. Mr. Jerry directed helpers and customers alike to hang firmly onto the outspread tarp.

"We've got you! Hang on just a moment longer." Together, the team stretched the tarp taut below Curtis. "Let go!"

"No way!" Curtis bellowed.

"Let go!" People chanted.

Whether Curtis let go or lost his grip no one could tell, but he plunged feet first toward the target. Patrick gaped at the scene before him as if it took place in slow motion. At the last second, Curtis leaned back with arms splayed to brace for impact. A piercing scream filled the air.

Zip! The sudden force ripped the tarp from the hands of several people.

Thud! Curtis struck the ground heavily. Silence. Dazed and bruised, he sat up and searched the crowd for Patrick.

"What happened?" Mr. Jerry inquired. "How did you end up crashing through the attic door?" He seemed more concerned than angry.

Curtis blubbered an answer, so Patrick stepped up and explained the incident. "So," he began, "when Curtis disappeared above me, I don't know what happened next."

"I—I noticed the sun shining through the cracks of the attic door, and when I tried to push it open, I fell through," Curtis finished the story.

Mr. Jerry glanced at the splinters of wood everywhere, shook his head, and motioned for everyone to return to business. Chad pulled the boys aside, quite aggravated at their behavior.

"Patrick and Curtis, you owe Mr. Jerry a sincere apology, and I expect you to pay for the broken attic door." He also took a good look at Curtis, his scrapes and bruises, and decided that he'd recover soon enough.

"Yes, Mr. Melberry," Curtis said.

"Okay, Dad. We're really sorry."

Chad spoke with Mr. Jerry, offering to pay for the repairs.

A little later, an elderly couple arrived at the yard sale and browsed for a bit. Then the gentleman asked Mr. Jerry if they could meet the mibsters and watch them shoot some marbles.

"Leigh, Alejandro, Patrick, come over here!" Mr. Jerry called. Alejandro, a boy from Mr. Jerry's competitive club rushed to him. Leigh found Patrick talking with Curtis and waved at him to join them.

"I didn't bring my marbles," Patrick said. "And I didn't qualify for nationals, so I don't think I should shoot."

"Nonsense," said Mr. Jerry.

"You can borrow one of my shooters," Leigh said.

The three boys cleared a patch in the dirt, drew a small circle and set the rack of thirteen marbles in place. Patrick took the break, the first shot of the game. Knocking a marble out of the ring, he shot again from the inside where his shooter had come to rest. Surprised at the immediate success, he hurried too fast and missed a tap shot, or a close marble. Patrick's turn ended. Alejandro took aim next.

"This brings me back to my childhood," the grey-haired man whispered to his wife. He rubbed his chin and gingerly kneeled down. "May I take a shot?" he asked.

"Sure!" Leigh said, handing the old man his aggie.

"A German-made agate! Just like my good ole' one." The guy steadied his hand, pinched the shooter with a seasoned grip, and flicked it with power and backspin.

"Wow!" Patrick was astonished.

The aggie brushed a mib but missed. "Ah," the gentleman stated, "I guess I need more practice." The mib spun in the dirt for a few seconds before coming to a rest. He struggled getting up and then reached in his pocket and withdrew his wallet.

"Sir," he spoke to Mr. Jerry, "Your yard sale sign said this is a fundraiser to send kids to a marble competition. Correct?"

Mr. Jerry gathered the three boys to his side describing each of them as good sports and great shooters. He pointed out that Alejandro and Leigh were competitors from Colorado and were going to the national tournament. Patrick felt important, nonetheless.

"I want to donate this," he said, handing a wad of folded bills to Mr. Jerry. "For bringing some joy into my life today." He thanked him and then shook hands with the boys, wishing them good luck.

Luck? Nope, attitude and skill, Patrick thought as he watched Mr. Jerry unroll the money. *One hundred dollars for a cherished, childhood pastime?* He pondered this and what it meant for him to play such an honored game.

CHAPTER 9

COLORADO INVITATIONAL

Chad and Deedee entered the quaint hotel, and Patrick followed behind feeling overjoyed. Rarely, did the Melberry family take hotel vacations, so this one was rather special. In combination, Patrick would participate in his first ever tournament, and he literally jiggled with jitters. Trying to sit still in the lobby, his feet rapidly tapped the floor sending vibrations up his chubby legs.

"Room 202," Chad said, slapping the card key on his palm.

"No elevator?" Deedee asked.

"I guess not," he answered. "No problem, grab our suitcases, and we'll take the stairs."

Patrick huffed and puffed after two trips up and down. He threw himself onto his bed and flipped on the television. Too nervous to watch, he pulled back the curtains to inspect the view. Across the highway was a beautiful park with trees and a fountain in the middle of a fishing pond that caused concentric ripples to spread toward the shore. He spied a corner of a concrete marbles pad, and his stomach flipped. Tomorrow, very early, he'd meet his opponents and the games would begin.

"Knock, knock!" Leigh's voice boomed from the other side of the door.

"Yesss," Patrick hissed happily.

"Let's go to the rings and practice," he suggested.

"Can I?" Patrick asked, looking to his parents.

"If you're safe," his mom replied. She worried about the weekend—safety, the weather, what the other moms might think of her, how they might judge Patrick's size, how long it would take, and would they get home too late?

Immediately, Patrick shoved his sock of marbles in his pocket and joined Leigh and some other kids from their club at the rings. It felt strange that Curtis wasn't with him. They'd done everything together, and now Patrick sensed a piece of himself was missing. *It's okay*, he told himself. *I'll see him in two days.*

Six sturdy concrete pads with perfect grey circles painted on each one filled a courtyard next to a covered ice hockey rink. Bleachers were on one side, big boulders on another, and freshly cut green grass surrounded the pads. Patrick counted eight picnic tables underneath a covered walkway. The late afternoon sun created speckled shadows from the aspen trees nearby, and he noticed a baseball game taking place in a distant field.

"Over here," Leigh shouted. "Let's practice lags first so we can get used to the surface."

"Yeah, I remember," Patrick said. "It's the first play of the game to see who goes first."

"In the gym, the pitch and taw lines were closer," Leigh said. "These aren't any different, just further apart."

Patrick recalled the lag where opponents stood behind a pitch line where they could either toss or roll their shooter toward the taw line on the opposite side. Whoever's shooter stopped closest to that line took the first break of the game.

Patrick couldn't explain what he felt when he stepped onto the marbles ring, but it hovered somewhere between fear and pride. He knelt down next to Leigh and counted: "One, two, three, lag," and then each sent their shooter toward the taw line. Patrick's bumble bee sped so swiftly across the circle that it slammed into the wooden border and bounced out of the pad itself.

"Thank goodness, we get practice lags," Leigh laughed. "Let's lag again."

This time, Patrick released his shooter gently, and it rolled toward the line, resting about a foot in front of it. He was pleased until he realized that Leigh's shooter sat within one inch of the line. So, Leigh set the marbles in the rack in the exact center of the ring and gently picked it up leaving the thirteen dark blue marbles a forever distance away from the edge of the circle from where he'd have to shoot. Lining up for the break shot, Leigh flicked his shooter next to his knee to practice backspin. Satisfied, he took his shot, knocking out two marbles. "Dubs!" he shouted.

"Dubs?"

"Two marbles out at a time is dubs and three out is trips," he explained. His shooter remained in the circle, so he took another close shot sending his target marble out. Again, he kept shooting until he hit a run of four, and his turn ended because his shooter left the ring.

"You're so awesome!" Patrick said. He figured he'd lose since seven marbles is a win, but Mrs. Lee always reminded the kids that the game is never over till it's actually over. Therefore, Patrick crouched down and aimed for the closest marble with some back up marbles just in case. Sure enough, he missed the nearest marble, but hit one behind it. His backspin had come a long way, but it wasn't enough to keep his bumble bee inside the circle.

Alejandro strolled over to say hello and asked how Curtis faired. He squinted at Leigh's aggie and screwed up his face. "He's good! He beat me in both games here last summer."

The three of them decided to practice together. They scattered all of their marbles in the ring. Taking turns, they practiced tap shots, or knocking marbles that sat fairly close together. The sun eventually dropped, and they struggled to knock the last three marbles out of the ring.

Patrick had spent the last hour and a half getting up and down repeatedly. His thighs burned, his back ached, and even the arches of his feet groaned from squatting on all fours. "Maybe we should quit. It's too dark to see," he said.

Alejandro agreed, but Leigh had marbles fever and refused to stop with only three to go. By this time, Patrick's dad came by looking for his son, who shivered from the cool breeze evaporating the sweat from his skin. He wished for a warm bed and a restful night's sleep, however, he and his dad huddled close until Leigh finally sent the last marble flying out of the circle.

"I need to work on my distance shots," Leigh commented, utterly wiped out. "I'll do better tomorrow." He shook Patrick's hand. "Thanks for hanging in there, buddy."

That night, Patrick tossed and turned in his sleep. His stomach had a thousand butterflies, his leg muscles cramped, and his back hurt. Never was he less ready for his first day of competition when the alarm sounded at 6:00 a.m.

"I'm awake, Dad," Patrick moaned. He literally rolled out of bed and onto the floor startling his mother.

"Oh, Pattycake! Are you alright? Is this tournament too much for you?"

"Mom!" Patrick said indignantly.

Minutes later, Patrick and his dad checked out the hotel's continental breakfast. His dad found the coffee, and Patrick grabbed several pastries. Deciding, three weren't enough, he snatched three more just as his mother entered the dining area.

"Pattycake, you'll get sick!" she whined. "Put some back."

Chad placed his hand on her waist and whispered something reassuring in her ear.

After breakfast, Patrick and his parents checked out of the hotel, drove the short block to the marbles rings and unloaded their gear—camp chairs, umbrellas, water jugs, sunscreen, and snacks. The parking lot already buzzed with new arrivals, kids Patrick didn't know, as well as some from his own club.

Mr. Jerry was busy taping sheets of paper to tables, unloading trophies, and setting up the scorekeeper's area. "The forecast shows a possible thunderstorm in the afternoon, so let's get this tournament going," he told a person holding a microphone. Patrick overheard his comment which made him feel even more anxious.

"Attention!" the announcer shouted. "All mibsters must check in at this time."

A mass of nervous children made a haphazard line in front of the announcer, who used a gauge to measure each shooter for legal size. He then sent them on to receive their nametags. Patrick held both his bumble bee and ugly black shooter in his already sweaty palm.

"They're legal," the announcer said. Patrick moved to the next table to receive his nametag, which he peeled off the sheet and stuck firmly on the front of his shirt.

Mrs. Lee prepared all the volunteer referees, but she would make the final calls on any disputed shots in the games. She left the scorer's table and visited with some kids and their parents whom Patrick had never met. Then she smiled cheerfully at Patrick.

"All of these players are as nervous as you are," she told Patrick. "If you smile, encourage them first, and remember sportsmanship above all, you'll have the best day ever," she said.

"Smile, shake hands, give compliments, thank the referees, have fun even if I don't win," Patrick said, repeating it again and again under his breath. The announcer called his name for a game. The contents of his stomach churned.

"On lag," the elderly referee said before counting: "One, two, three, lag."

Patrick's bumble bee rolled a few feet and stopped. The second lag counted, so he let go with more gusto the second time and won the lag. A boy about his age with a name tag reading Titus dropped his head. Patrick stepped up, took his hand, and said, "You're going to do well."

The boy's eyes lit up with glee. "Thanks."

They played the full six innings, meaning they each took six turns shooting. Patrick won the first game four to two, but Titus scored three while Patrick hit nothing out during the second game.

"One match down, twelve to go," Patrick's dad said, patting him on the back.

"Twenty-six games might be the death of me, Dad. Don't remind me," Patrick said feeling pleased and discouraged at the same time.

His mom looked worried—about everything.

Halfway through the morning, Patrick was paired up with Alejandro, who rejoiced at his day's winnings so far. "How many games have you won, Patrick?"

"Uh, not a lot."

"It's okay. It's your first tournament."

Patrick thought that maybe Alejandro shouldn't brag, but he shook hands sincerely anyway. Unfortunately, he lost the lag, and Alejandro slaughtered him mercilessly in both games.

Thankfully, the announcer called a break so the mini mibsters tournament could take place. The circles were reduced to five feet in diameter for the little tykes. To Patrick it looked like some of the mini mibsters were babies, but Mrs. Lee reassured him that one was two and the other was three years old. The rest were up to five years old. Families gathered around to watch as their tiny tots were given a coach—an experienced, older player—to guide them through the games.

More cheers rose up in the mini mibsters tournament than Patrick had witnessed all morning. He couldn't help but laugh as he rooted them on as well. They were so cute with their silliness. A little girl, who could hardly hold the shooter in her miniature hands ended up tossing it into the ring. The two-year-old wanted his mommy, and an adorable child kept throwing kisses to the audience. Somehow, one kid ended up winning the tournament by actually hitting a total of ten marbles out of the circle over a series of games.

"How refreshing!" Deedee said smiling for the first time that day. "I'm so glad to see these youngsters involved."

At that, another mom started up a conversation with her, and Patrick felt a weight drop from his shoulders. He hadn't realized he'd been carrying all of her concerns and worries around up to this point. He found Leigh who was practicing his backspin. "We play against each other next," Patrick said.

"I like to think of it as we play *together* next," Leigh said grinning.

A corny referee kept cracking jokes during their games, and even though Patrick lost to Leigh, he decided that having fun meant a whole lot more to him than winning. In fact, when he relaxed, he shot better. As the number of games being played dwindled, Patrick made it his purpose to see to it that his opponents left the rings happy no matter what.

During the most incredible lunch of pulled pork, watermelon, salad, and dessert, dark clouds started gathering in the southwest. Patrick thanked the parents who prepared that meal, and Patrick filled himself to the brim thanking them more than once for it. Mr. Jerry cut lunch short so they might finish the tournament before the storm arrived.

What occurred next was the most incredible marbles shooting Patrick had ever witnessed. Former national competitors—including two for real national champions—and national best sport award winners, apparently all from Colorado, demonstrated astonishing skills. A tiny airsoft pellet was placed in the center of the ring, and both of the national champs and one other mibster knocked it out on their first try. In addition, a girl of about sixteen, took aim at the rack of thirteen and continued to tap out seven marbles in a row—which is called a stick, as Mrs. Lee explained, and is considered a perfect game. Patrick glanced at Leigh who seemed entranced.

Patrick only needed to play three more matches, but with a full belly, blisters on his fingers, and a lapse of time, he struggled to push himself. "Marbles is definitely a sport, because I'm sore," he told his parents.

Patrick's mom couldn't decide if she should rejoice that her son spent the day doing a sound marbles workout or if she should pull him out of the tournament.

"Get out there, son, and finish strong," his dad said.

"Ugh." He suddenly didn't feel strong. Instead, he felt exhausted, worn out, beat up. His muscles screamed, and the blisters stung. Noticing holes in his pants, he rolled them up and spotted red sores on both knees. Yet, he forced himself to tread to the ring where Mrs. Lee refereed his next game.

"I'm proud of you, Patrick," she said before his opponent arrived.

That filled his tank, and he knew he'd make it the rest of the way. Just then, a distant bolt of lightning scorched the sky followed by a rumble of thunder and then a light pattering of raindrops.

"Keep the games rolling," Mr. Jerry announced over the microphone. "Unless the lightning moves in, we'll play in the rain."

Most of the audience shifted to the covered picnic area. A few referees put on rain gear, and Mrs. Lee handed out dish rags.

"What's this for?" Patrick asked.

"Keep your fingers and shooter dry," she replied.

Of course, other sports take place in the rain—why not marbles? Patrick tucked his rag under his shirt and pulled it out before each shot. He found that he enjoyed a wet ring because with his power shots, the shooter didn't roll out as fast. Surprised, he won both games, knocking out a total of eight marbles, the most he'd scored in a match so far.

The tournament ended just as the thunder and lightning seized the sky. Heavy drops pounded the rings, leaving little rivers between the six marble pads and creating a soppy, wet mess of the dirt and grass surrounding them. The awards ceremony would transpire under cover where Mr. Jerry and Mrs. Lee already transferred the awards and prizes. The scorekeeper, a tech-savvy guy, double-checked all the results and then handed Mr. Jerry an official printout.

The former national competitors passed gift bags and participant ribbons to each mibster then place trophies were awarded. Patrick knew he wouldn't get a prize, but he wondered if Leigh or Alejandro would win first place.

"With a score of one hundred twenty-one marbles, our second-place winner is Leigh!"

Patrick hooted and hollered with congratulations as Leigh accepted his trophy and stood patiently for photos.

"And in first place with a total of one hundred twenty-four marbles is Alejandro!"

More cheers and clapping.

Mrs. Lee picked up one last trophy, a coveted award that she described as the reason she coached kids, and the one that characterized a true mibster. She spoke deliberately into the microphone, "This year's best sport award goes to—" she said choking up just a little—"to Patrick!"

The crowd erupted into applause, and strangers shook Patrick's hand, rubbed his arms, and hugged him. "You never gave up." "Thanks for encouraging Titus." "You smiled even when you lost." The compliments kept coming.

Deedee cried, wiping the smudged makeup from her eyes.

Chad embraced his son.

Leigh posed for pictures with his teammate and friend.

And Patrick felt numb.

CHAPTER 10

END OF SUMMER

"You really won Best Sport?" Curtis guffawed.

"Yeah, I did!" Patrick answered, punching Curtis's shoulder just hard enough to make a point.

Curtis changed his tone. "Well, that's awesome then."

Just a few short weeks of summer lay ahead of them, and Curtis was restless. "Get a bike, Patrick, so we can ride."

"Um."

"Seriously, let's ask your mom," Curtis said pointedly, already heading inside Patrick's house. Finding her in the kitchen Curtis called out, "Mrs. Melberry, Patrick wants a bike."

Patrick's jaw dropped.

"Finally!" she shouted. "How *ever* did you talk him into this, Curtis?" Deedee dropped her hand towel and hugged him.

"Mom, I—"

"My dad says there's a bicycle sale at the hardware store today," Curtis interrupted. "We should go before they sell out."

"I agree," Deedee said. "What're we waiting for?"

Patrick glared at Curtis who brushed it aside.

Arriving at the store, a series of bikes lined the parking lot.

Customers seemed to wheel them off at a surprising speed. "Hurry, boys," Deedee said.

"I don't want a bike," Patrick muttered to Curtis.

"Yes, you do. It'll be fun," Curtis said.

An employee asked who would be riding the new bicycle. Deedee pointed at her son, and then caught the reaction of the salesperson. "Has he owned a bike, previously?" she asked doubtfully.

"No, but he has ridden before," she answered in embarrassment.

Patrick felt humiliated.

"How about this one?" Curtis grabbed the handlebars of a sturdy boys' bike.

Patrick frowned.

"Try it, Pattycake," Patrick's mom commanded.

"Geez," he said, trying to steady the bike so he could lift his plump leg over the bar. No luck.

The employee shook her head. "May I suggest this somewhat masculine-looking girl's bike?" Dark green, with only a few fancy swirls, the saleswoman attempted to cover the rosy, pink seat with her elbow and forearm.

"No!" Patrick grimaced.

"Don't say no until you've tried it," his mom said. "Without a bar, you should feel more comfortable."

Can this get any worse? Patrick wondered.

Ten minutes later, after Patrick clumsily pedaled the bicycle several feet without once sitting on that mortifying seat, Deedee said, "We'll take it." After paying the salesperson, she pushed the despised green hunk of metal into the van and drove home. After numerous attempts to get Patrick to go riding, Curtis gave up and left.

Patrick overheard his parents carrying on that evening about his mom's new purchase. "He wanted one. He couldn't lift his leg over the bar, so I bought a girl's bike," his mom said matter-of-factly.

"With a pink seat!" his dad replied with a raised voice.

"When he sits down on it, no one will notice," she argued.

"Patrick will!"

"Well, I can't return it. It's a sale item."

His dad grumbled, and the discussion ended.

The very next day, Patrick's dad went out and bought a padded black seat. After replacing the too-small pink one, Patrick agreed to test out the bike in the alley. "If you truly detest this," his dad said, "I'll sell it. However, I sometimes rode my sister's bike when I was your age, and I can't begin to tell you the fun I had."

"Okay, Dad." Patrick balanced on the seat uncomfortably at first. He felt squishy as his bulging lumps slumped over the edges. He shifted and squirmed. Positioning his feet on the peddles, he pushed his right foot down. Wobbling, he managed to gain enough speed to keep the bike up for a few yards. Finally, Patrick tested the brakes, and the bicycle obeyed. He peeled his plump rear end off of the seat, pushed the bike back to the garage and parked it. "That's enough for today."

Several days later, hardly believing he had agreed to do this, Patrick pedaled his bike some ways behind Curtis. They reached their destination to Patrick's relief. His heart was pumping way too fast, and he was breathing rapidly. He leaned the bike against a brick wall and bent over to catch his breath.

"See those girls over there?" Curtis pointed.

He looked up. "Yeah."

"Watch!" Curtis pumped the pedals and raced in the direction of the young ladies. Just before he was going to run into them, he whipped around sending a spray of rocks in their direction. The girls shouted and shook their fists at him, but he swung around again going full speed, creating a dirt cloud from his whirling tires. The girls ran, screaming insults at him.

Patrick snorted with laughter at first but then his smile turned to a look of concern as he felt somewhat dismayed.

"No one got hurt, Patrick," Curtis said reacting to Patrick's countenance.

"I know," Patrick said, seeing Curtis's slight sense of shame.

"I won't bother them again. Let's go ride by the river," Curtis said.

Casting stones into the water, the boys reminisced about fourth grade. Both of them anticipated their fifth grade year with dread and excitement.

"I hope we're in the same class," Curtis spoke up.

"Me, too!" Patrick hadn't imagined any other scenario.

"What should we do with our bubble gum this year?" Curtis pretended to fill his mouth and chew. He grinned mischievously.

"Hmmm," the thought rattled around in Patrick's mind. "We better start planning that one."

Ben's family always held a back-to-school party at their house. He invited many of their friends and neighbors but not Patrick and Curtis. They could hear the festivities a block away from Patrick's home.

"Not that I hate school," Curtis said, "but parties should celebrate the end of the year not the beginning."

"Right!" Patrick agreed. He wondered what horrible nickname TJ and Ben would assign him this year. "We should crash their party."

"I have a better idea!" Curtis tapped his head. "Remember last year, after Ben's party? He dumped all the half-eaten watermelon rinds in your front yard?"

"My mom was furious!"

"We have a cantaloupe at my house," Curtis said. "And it's ripe."

"Yeah?"

"Can you sneak out tonight?" Curtis asked.

"After my dad goes to bed, yes!" Patrick replied. He wouldn't miss Curtis's spectacular prank for the world, especially if it was revengeful.

"Okay, tap my bedroom window tonight," said Curtis.

"Got it!"

Anticipation welled up while Patrick counted the minutes until he suspected his dad would nod off. Finally, sometime after 11:00 p.m., he tip-toed through the kitchen and out the back door. With practice, he'd become quite successful at this exit procedure. Padding through the alley, just two houses down, he arrived at Curtis's window.

Tap, tap. No response.

Tap, tap, a little harder this time. Still no answer.

His foot bumped into a closed box. Patrick read a scribbled note. "I got in trouble for talking back to my mom, so she put me on house arrest. My window alarm will beep, so I can't sneak out. Don't worry. It's all here and ready to go. Sorry. Oh, and burn this note and throw away the evidence."

In the box was a very ripe cantaloupe with holes dug into it, a thick straw, funnel, and a water bottle. *What?* Patrick contemplated. Curtis hadn't filled him in on his prank. Standing up with the box, he traipsed toward the alley and to Ben's house.

Puzzled, he inspected the items once again. The straw fit tightly into one of the holes. "Now what?" Opening the water bottle, he took a whiff of the contents and choked. Vinegar! Recalling Mr. Seitler's volcano experiment, he appreciated Curtis's plan. He suspected the interior of the cantaloupe had been stuffed with baking soda, somehow. He let go a naughty snicker and proceeded to prowl around the exterior of Ben's house.

He prayed that the open window belonged to Ben, nonetheless, he tested the loose screen and decided with enough pull it would release. First, Patrick searched for an escape route down the alley, then he turned to his business.

Grunting, he grasped a tab on the screen and yanked as softly as he could, a scraping sound kept him frozen for a few seconds. Again, he pinched the tab, lifted slightly, and clink! It created a barely audible squeak as he slid the screen enough to leave a sizeable space. Patrick wished Curtis hadn't been dumb enough to get in trouble, because his nerves just lit up like a firecracker.

He fumbled with the funnel, then finally shoved it onto the straw which stuck crookedly out of the cantaloupe. The vinegar burned his nostrils enough to make him want to cough. He swallowed hard. Then, expeditiously, he poured the liquid down the funnel and through the straw, gave it a good shake as snakes of effervescence squirted out the holes. Immediately, Patrick pitched the gathering time bomb through the window and darted as fast as his chubby legs would carry him.

"Oh no, dummy!" he chided himself. Patrick left the evidence under the window. No going back now as shrieks resounded inside the house—not Ben's voice, he realized. Maybe his sister or his mom, Patrick wasn't sure, but from the screams, it sounded as if the cantaloupe erupted just like the volcano. Unable to control himself, he burst out laughing, quite certain his guffaws weren't heard amidst the commotion within the house.

Patrick stuffed Curtis's note in his mouth and chewed it like a pack of bubble gum until he swallowed chunk after chunk. Silently nudging the back door, he stepped inside, crept to his room, crawled in his bed, and grinned. Although he stilled smelled of vinegar, he soon fell sound asleep.

Patrick awoke to his dad's phone whistling a notification. "Hello," Chad answered. "I'm sorry to hear that." A long pause later, "I'll let my son know."

Patrick sat up in bed pretending to rub his eyes, although he was wide awake with curiosity and dread. His dad walked into his room frowning.

"Son, your friend, Curtis, has been accused of causing damage to a neighbor's house—something about a broken screen, and an explosion." His dad shook his head. "It happened in the middle of the night last night."

"Oh gosh!" Patrick acted shocked. "Why Curtis?"

"The police remarked that a boy named Ben insisted that Curtis hated him and intended to cause his family harm."

"They called the cops?" Patrick shoved his shaking hands under the covers. "What happened to Curtis?"

"His dad just called me and declared that Curtis was innocent of all accusations as he'd been under surveillance all night, and they could prove it!" Patrick's dad said.

"Uh, he's probably right. His mom put an alarm system in his room so Curtis wouldn't try to leave when he had time-outs," Patrick explained, leaving out the part about sneaking out at nights.

"I'm certain everything will work out, son. The officers will do a thorough investigation," his dad said, gently ruffling Patrick's hair.

He fell face first into his pillow, imagining the worst.

CHAPTER 11

FIFTH GRADE

The investigation petered out a week later when the police concluded that Curtis had indeed spent the night in his room under guard. One officer spoke with Chad and Deedee, but they reassured him that Patrick was a good kid who couldn't possibly pull off a stunt like that. Deedee even went so far as to discuss his weight and inability to run from the scene without being detected. Apparently, the officer was satisfied, and the case was closed.

"Whew!" Curtis sighed as he slobbered, the juicy wad of gum slipping out his mouth.

"We're lucky, Curtis!" Patrick said. "We could've been arrested."

"Nah," Curtis slurped. "Ben does stupid stuff too. His parents probably figured that he'd had a fight with his sister and played the prank on her."

"I guess. Ready?" Patrick tossed his backpack over his shoulder.

"Yep."

Upon his first step on the playground, Curtis took off in a sprint, disappeared around the building, and returned just as swiftly. His hair had grown long over the summer, and it splayed out around his face, looking like a lion's mane. His green eyes twinkled rascally.

"Your gum?" Patrick asked.

"Stuck right where the latch meets the faceplate in our classroom door," Curtis beamed. "What about you?"

"I'm going to fill TJ's or Ben's pencil box."

A woman whom neither boy knew stood at the entrance to fifth grade. They glanced at each other and shrugged their shoulders, assuming an instructional assistant welcomed them in.

Patrick dropped his backpack by the coatracks and shuffled around the room. There were no nametags at the seats. Students meandered here and there waiting for directions.

"Take a seat!" the woman called out.

Patrick rushed toward the back of the room with Curtis on his heels. "Awesome! The first year ever we get to sit together!"

"Quiet, everyone!" she yelled. "I'm Ms. Hedgewick, your teacher this year. Mrs. Granby delivered her baby over the summer and chose to take a leave of absence."

Celia squealed with delight in hearing about the birth.

"I run a strict classroom," Ms. Hedgewick growled. "You had all best learn that as soon as possible." She strolled between the aisles taking a head count.

"You," she said as she stopped and directed her intense gaze at Patrick.

"Uh, me?" Patrick trembled.

"Spit that hunk of gum into the trash this very second!"

"I—I don't—"

"What's your name?" she spoke feverishly.

"P—Patrick Melberry," he whispered.

"After you dump your gum in the wastebasket, take that seat right up there by my desk," she ordered.

TJ and Ben snickered from somewhere in the classroom.

His gum plopped to the bottom of the trash can with a thud.

Then he plopped unhappily into his seat. Patrick glowered as he stared at his desk thinking, *I can't stand her already*.

Students fidgeted nervously as the morning passed without even a bathroom break or a chance to stand and stretch. Patrick desperately wanted to peer behind him hoping to catch a glimpse of Curtis, but he remained uncomfortably glued to his chair.

Eventually, Ms. Hedgewick's drone dissipated, and after being forced to stand in a straight line, she dismissed them for recess. Sighs of relief escaped the lungs of the fifth graders as they rushed outside. Even Patrick eagerly greeted this recess with enthusiasm.

"If I still had my gum, I'd wrap it around her neck and pull hard," Patrick said. "She's awful!"

"She's a witch!" Curtis blared. "Ms. Hedge*witch*." He slumped to the dirt below the shade tree and pouted.

TJ, Ben, and a new kid, Carlos, strutted over. Ben spoke up. "I don't know how you did it, but I know you blew up that cantaloupe, and you're going to pay for it."

"Speaking of blowing up," TJ pointed at Patrick. "Is it even possible that you're fatter this year than last?"

The new kid cackled. "You're the most enormous cow I've ever seen!"

Curtis jerked himself up and took two brisk steps toward TJ. His face was screwed up and his eyes shot daggers at them. "I've never been in a fight, but I guarantee you that if you threaten me or Patrick again, I'll tear your skin right off your bones and leave you shaking where you stand!"

Surprised at Curtis's aggressive reaction, the three boys backed away. Then TJ yelled from a distance, "Patrick-cow!"

Curtis bolted, overtook TJ, and shoved him to the ground. "Maybe you haven't noticed who's the taller, stronger kid this year." In reality, he *had* grown over the summer, and even his boyish arms showed some muscles.

"I'm telling our teacher," TJ cried as he ran toward his friends.

"Boo-hoo," Patrick whined right back.

Recess ended too soon. The students lined up at their door, and that's when Patrick realized that Gail was nowhere to be seen. He searched the group of kids entering the other fifth grade classroom. Maybe he missed her already having had no chance to inspect the students in his class this year. Spying his seat, he looked dejectedly at it, then sunk down and just hoped the day would end.

When the final bell rang, freeing them from class, Curtis came up to Patrick and said, "She's in the other fifth grade class. Gail, I saw her."

"That stinks," replied Patrick.

"Sure does," Curtis said. He and Patrick trudged home, hating a huge part of that day.

"Come in, Curtis," suggested Patrick's mom as he stepped inside. "I've just removed cookies from the oven."

Maybe there's still hope for the day, Patrick thought.

The boys ate their frustrations away and eventually melted onto the couch watching cartoons.

"I better go home," Curtis announced, "before my mom gets off work. See you tomorrow, Patrick."

Patrick felt certain that Curtis's mom and Ms. Hedgewick were related somehow.

Monday finally arrived, and so did Marbles for Fun Club. Patrick met Leigh at the gym door, and they greeted each other with a hug.

"I have so much to tell you about the national tournament!" Leigh said. "I'm going back!"

"You already know that?" asked Patrick.

"I'm planning on practicing every day," Leigh answered.

Mrs. Lee smiled sweetly as she joined a rather large group around the circle. "Welcome to Marbles Club!" she exclaimed and then went on to remind the students of the expectations. Everyone received shiny, new mibs and a shooter. Then she announced the game. "It's called Corner the Cow."

Patrick's jaw dropped and his heart sank right to the floor. *Is she in on it too?* he wondered. His imagination rushed into a horrendous scenario of everyone in the club chasing him into a corner and shooting bullets at him with their marbles. He left his trance in time to watch her hold a small boulder of a marble up for all to observe.

"A larger marble, such as this one," Mrs. Lee said, "has many names—boulder, bumboozer, giant, or even cow." Everyone oohed and aahed.

Patrick selected Leigh as a partner so he could hear about nationals. During their game, he learned that Leigh took twelfth place out of twenty-nine boys. He described the sandy rings and the distractions from the boardwalk. Leigh also talked about hunching, a new term that some people used.

"What's that?" Patrick asked.

"It's like a foul. If you lift your hand from the ring when shooting, it's called Scrumpy Knuckles." Leigh smiled. Most of the time people refer to it as hunching, but I think the other name is funny." Leigh then looked at Patrick intently and said, "I'm going to make it to semi-finals next year, Patrick."

"I want to go too," Patrick blurted. "I'm just not good enough."

"I'll practice with you and help you. I promise."

In class the next morning, Ms. Hedgewick assigned a writing project due that day. "Where do you see yourself five years from now?" she asked, making it clear she wouldn't accept a joking answer.

Patrick's mind traveled to the national marbles tournament. He titled his essay Scrumpy Knuckles and proceeded to write his dreams. Carlos, the new kid, was passing by his desk when he slowed to peek at Patrick's paper. Chuckling, he moved on to the pencil sharpener.

Carlos was from Mexico and was athletic, especially in soccer. With jet black hair, deep set brown eyes, and a flashing white-toothed smile, he was popular with the girls too. He spoke fluent Spanish and at first cussed in Spanish in class. The school administrator was also bilingual, and called Carlos into his office the first day. After that, he only cussed to impress TJ and Ben.

After lunch one day, TJ cornered Patrick by the coatrack. "Carlos isn't afraid to fight Curtis," TJ told him. "Keep that in mind, you stupid, fat cow. You're too huge to play any other sport, so you join a baby's club because you can't catch a football or baseball with those pudgy fingers of yours." He paused and then said, "Patrick, Pudgy Knuckles."

He moved to lash out at TJ, but Ms. Hedgewick poked her nose into their business. "Boys, enough! Take your seats this instance!"

Patrick's blood boiled. One way or another, he intended to take revenge on TJ *and* Ms. Hedgewick.

The week dragged on and Patrick continued to stew in his anger. Curtis wasn't his usual self either, so by the time the Friday afternoon bell rang, they both felt like prisoners breaking free. However, TJ and Carlos didn't leave with the bus riders. Instead, they hung around talking to Ben and watching Curtis and Patrick.

"Hey, they're walking today," Curtis whispered.

"Yeah, same as us," Patrick snarled.

"Wait a minute. Let's see which way they go," Curtis said, pulling Patrick toward him. After a minute, Curtis nudged his friend, and the two of them chose an alternate route. They didn't fear the bullies, but they hoped to catch them off guard. From somewhere close, they heard TJ's cackling and Carlos responding sarcastically and then silence.

"Why did it get quiet?" Patrick murmured.

Curtis glanced around.

Like prowling lions, Carlos leapt at Curtis's legs while Ben inched toward Patrick. TJ stood his ground just in case.

Immediately, Curtis crashed to the ground fists swinging

wildly while Carlos twisted into an offensive position like an experienced wrestler. He whacked Curtis in the jaw. Suddenly, Patrick got a surge of adrenaline, and he threw himself into the middle of the fight, punching and kicking. They exchanged blows and then, Curtis shouted, "Let go, you leech!" The three of them grappled in the dirt for a few minutes. Curtis wrenched himself free from Carlos's grasp and Patrick's overbearing weight. He then turned on the other two. "You're next, Ben. Come on!" His wild hair was in disarray and his wiry muscles bulged ready for an attack.

Somehow Patrick flung Carlos flat on his back, bending his arm awkwardly beneath his body. With the other arm, Carlos pinched and scratched Patrick with all his might, but he wouldn't relent. He wrapped his large legs across his enemy's knees and pushed Carlos's flailing arm into the dirt. He pressed all of his weight on Carlos's torso.

Carlos panted, "Help!"

TJ shouted a warning, "Get off him, you freak! He can't breathe!"

"Make him!" Curtis screeched, spitting red saliva.

Ben took a step forward, and Curtis swung his fist inches from his face. "Go ahead and try, Barf bag!" Curtis yelled. He attempted another blow, but Ben retreated.

TJ lost his composure and started bawling and begging Patrick not to kill his friend. Ben panicked, thinking the worst. Finally, Patrick rolled off Carlos's limp body, kneeled down next to him and spit in the dirt.

"Cow, one. Carlos, zero," Patrick said, breathing heavily.

Curtis walked over to Carlos, who was sucking air into his lungs, and said "Not dead, after all."

Carlos rotated to his hands and knees and motioned for his friends to help him up. They did so hesitantly for fear of assault, but Curtis positioned himself next to Patrick, who was grinning from ear to ear.

"Don't ever come after us again!" hollered Curtis as the boys scurried off.

Patrick sized up his friend's injuries and concluded that he received the brunt of the battle. Curtis bled from his lips and mouth, his purple cheek swelled, and he had a torn sleeve with raw skin underneath.

"You should see *yourself*," Curtis deflected. "A crazy cat clawed you up. Take your shirt off."

"No. Why?"

"Check out the scratches," Curtis said, raising the shirt.

"Dang!" he smiled. "My mom might just rush me to the hospital."

Curtis laughed. "She just might."

A bond deeper than blood was formed that day.

CHAPTER 12

LEIGH

"So, what did your parents do after the fight?" asked Leigh as he flicked his shooter.

"My mom sort of freaked out, but my dad convinced her not to press charges. He told her to let the whole event blow over," Patrick said. "She wouldn't talk to him for two whole days. Ha, they're better now, though."

Leigh positioned his body, spun his aggie one more time, then aimed at a marble three feet inside the circle. Smack! The mib zipped out of the ring, and his agate spun off to the right. "Mrs. Lee gave me a list of shots to practice instead of just playing Ringer over and over. Honestly, it's boring, but my tap shots have improved."

Patrick dumped his sock of marbles and searched for his bumble bee.

"Use the ugly black one," Leigh told him. "You'll need to get used to the roughness."

"I don't like that one," Patrick complained, but he grabbed it anyway.

"Here's the list. Since we're together, maybe it'll be more fun," Leigh said. As usual, he exuded positivity.

At the park, the three concrete pads had seen some use, and not just from the mibsters. Leigh had swept branches and leaves off of them earlier, and now Patrick smashed a flood of sugar ants under his foot. Someone had drawn pink chalk hearts on one ring. Sticky soda splattered another ring. They chose the one under the shade tree with the falling leaves for Leigh to keep his promise to help Patrick work his way to nationals.

"Oh, yeah, I forgot," Leigh said, reaching into his pocket. "These are eleven marbles for your eleventh birthday tomorrow. My dad says they're antique, so here you go."

"Cool! That's what I asked my parents for, for my birthday." He inspected the crockeries—old, clay spheres covered in a glaze of some kind, and baked in a fiery furnace. "Thanks, Leigh!"

"You're welcome. Don't shoot with them though. Add them to you ever-growing collection."

"Knuckles down," Patrick used the term for the beginning of marbles play. He drew ten chalk lines two inches apart like a ladder. Commencing, he put a target mib on the first line and set to work hitting it ten times in a row. Then, much later, he did the same on the second row.

Leigh picked up a piece of chalk and drew a six-inch circle around each of his lines. "In order to make semi-finals, I need to hit each marble off each line and make my shooter sit spinning inside these little circles."

Patrick looked at him dumbfounded. "Well, what do *I* need to do just to make it to nationals?"

"Mrs. Lee says to be able to hit fifty percent of all the marbles you aim at," Leigh explained. Seeing Patrick's shocked face, he added, "And that's why I'm practicing with you." Then, he knelt down and studied Patrick's grip and aim, showing him how to straighten his wrist and adjust his shooter between his thumb and index finger to control the amount of spin.

Patrick thought his thumb would never stop stinging that evening. His callous didn't compare to Leigh's, at least not yet. Nevertheless, they planned to meet at the park every Wednesday for two hours until winter, and then they'd practice in Leigh's garage where his dad had painted a sandy ring on the smooth, cement floor. Leigh also explained the necessity of practicing every day in the spring.

In between practices, school, and Marbles Club, Curtis and Patrick passed the time riding bikes to the river and along nearby trails. The bullies had left them alone for the most part but tensions still arose during the tedious classroom times when Ms. Hedgewick was on a witchy roll. They were always on edge just waiting for her nasty mood to flood the fifth grade room. Those days brought out the worst in everyone.

It was after one of those days, on a Wednesday, when the boys met at the park and Patrick's frustrations kept flaring up. "I'm missing every one!" He slumped down on the ring. "Why can't I be like you?" he asked Leigh.

"You will. Just keep practicing."

"That's not what I mean. You're not just great at marbles. You're always happy and everybody likes you." Patrick said.

Leigh picked up his shooter. "I'm not a popular guy at school, Patrick. My friends and I—we don't fit in with that crowd. They have worldly values."

"It's because you're a mibster, isn't it?" Patrick shook his head.

"No, it's not that. It's because I'm a believer," Leigh answered.

Confused, Patrick asked, "What does that mean?"

"I believe in Jesus as my Savior. I don't cuss, and I read my Bible at school. People make fun of me for it."

"I—I didn't know that." He thought for a moment. "I don't know anything about Jesus, but I sure understand how it feels to be teased."

"You're heavy and that's all people see, but you're more important than how you look," Leigh said.

"I doubt that." Patrick commented. "I'd be worth a lot more if I wasn't fat!"

"You won the best sport award at the state competition for encouraging others and not giving up, but you have tons to learn about respecting yourself," Leigh chided him. "Do you want to practice or put yourself down?"

Humiliated by someone he admired left Patrick feeling like trash. "I'd rather go home."

"Half of the game is ability, and the other half is attitude. The same can be said about life. God gave you talents, but if all you do is complain, then you won't ever reach your potential."

"Is that a quote? Where did you hear it?" Patrick questioned him.

"When I first started playing marbles, I got so mad when I missed. I threw mibs and even walked away from games pouting." He stared at Patrick. "Mrs. Lee told me I couldn't be in Marbles Club anymore if I acted that way. She threatened to kick me out."

"Mrs. Lee? No way!"

"She said negative attitudes don't allow our God-given talents to grow," replied Leigh. "So I tried harder, and she let me stay in the club." He smiled. "Mrs. Lee wrote that quote on a card and asked me to memorize it because it might come in handy someday."

"Handy for me, I guess." Patrick swallowed hard. "Okay, I'll practice."

After two hours of repeatedly missing shots, Patrick rubbed his sore thumb and wiped the chalk lines from the ring. "Leigh, how *did* you change your attitude?"

"Um, well, someone taught me about Jesus. Then, I guess I just started believing in him myself," Leigh grinned, shrugging his shoulders. "I'm tired today, but ask me again next week, and I'll give you a better answer."

Curtis showed up at Patrick's house fairly early Friday morning. "Eat these," he said, handing him a squishy bag of mottled beans.

"Why?"

"They'll make us fart and fart and fart!"

Patrick dumped a good portion of the bag in his mouth and steadily chewed the soft beans before swallowing them. Finishing his bag before Curtis, he belched loudly. "How long before the farts come?"

"We ate these for dinner last night, and before I went to bed, I took a bubble bath if you know what I mean," Curtis replied. "By this afternoon, we should be putting on quite a show."

Ms. Hedgewick had invited a guest speaker that afternoon. She ordered them to group together on the floor to view the specimens he brought. Her admonitions sent shivers up the spines of her students, and the entire class sat dutifully still while the guest talked about bird banding. Curtis sat near Celia, a popular girl who disliked him most of the time. Patrick purposefully scrunched between TJ and Ben who muttered obscenities under their breaths yet didn't dare make a fuss with the witch watching.

"We've managed to net several species of finch and fasten these bands—"

Suddenly a sound of emitting gas rang out. The speaker stopped at the sound and passed a questioning glance at the teacher.

Ms. Hedgewick pinched her lips and motioned for him to continue.

Curtis cut the cheese again slowly allowing the sound to resonate and the odor to permeate the air.

Kids squirmed and pinched their noses.

Taking turns, the two boys farted, tooted, and passed so much gas that the air became noxious. Ms. Hedgewick snarled as she searched the class for the culprits while encouraging her guest to keep talking.

The speaker appeared to finish unexpectedly. Then he requested comments from the class.

Patrick held it for this opportune time. Right before anyone said anything, he let go a reverberating wind that sounded like a muffled tuba as it bubbled up and out from under his rear end. TJ gagged and Ben bent over to cover his face with his shirt. Patrick acted as if nothing had happened and paid close attention to the bird guy.

Ms. Hedgewick seethed. Her eyes bulged and her lips were pressed together so tightly they turned white. Ears glowing red and hot under the collar, her silent fuming could've set the gaseous air on fire. Patrick wished he had a lighter. Oh, how he desired to watch her lose control, go raving mad, and possibly get fired.

Despite her gritted teeth and clenched fists, Ms. Hedgewick managed to acknowledge the guest, demand that the class thank him in unison, and then ordered them outside for an unplanned recess. They happily and readily obeyed.

The students chattered amongst themselves, wondering who the offenders were and often accusing each other or a classmate at random.

TJ pointed at the culprit. "You!"

"Who me?" Patrick asked nonchalantly.

"You sat right next to me! You stink like cow manure!"

"Prove it," Patrick responded indignantly.

Curtis gleefully let go fart after fart, not holding back out of embarrassment or shame. "Beans, beans, the magical fruit, the more you eat, the more you toot," he sang.

Ms. Hedgewick made her way outside and sucked in as much fresh air as possible. "You evil children! How dare you treat our guest in this manner," she yelled at no one in particular. Growling like a rabid dog, she barked, "Ten minutes more and then you'll be punished for your behavior!"

Celia walked toward Curtis and said, "You're weird, Curtis, but she's crazy!"

"Huh?" he responded, a little surprised.

"You fart for fun, but no teacher should punish her students just because someone has gas," Celia stated. "I'm going to tell the principal, and I want you to admit that you passed wind."

"Go with you, to the principal?"

"Yes, weirdo," Celia said.

They snuck around the side of the building and out of Patrick's sight.

When Ms. Hedgewick called her students back to class, she glowered at each one as they passed her in the doorway. The room smelled like disinfectant spray. Patrick had forced his farts to remain quiet till he could use the restroom, but in the meantime, the teacher began to berate them. Just then, Curtis, Celia and the principal entered. He asked to speak to the teacher alone for a moment.

The whispering stopped when the principal re-entered the classroom. He announced that Ms. Hedgewick didn't feel well, so he released her for the rest of the day. He suggested they work on homework or free read till the bell rang.

"So, did she get fired?" Leigh asked, picking up the rack and scattered marbles.

"I don't know. We've had a substitute this week," Patrick replied. "Leigh, I have a question."

"Yeah?"

"When you miss shots nowadays, you don't get mad. What do you tell yourself so you can keep shooting?"

"I pray and ask Jesus for help."

"Jesus helps you shoot?" he asked befuddled. "Was he a good marbles player or something?"

"That's funny," Leigh chuckled. "He probably shot marbles in his time, but that's not what I pray about."

"Well, then, what do you pray about?"

"He tells me that if I play to honor him, I'll shoot better. He gives me the confidence to keep a good attitude no matter what." Leigh flicked his aggie. "I ask him to be with me."

Patrick mulled it over for a while, watching Leigh's backspin.

"I don't think Jesus would help me. I've done too many bad things," Patrick said.

"You'd be surprised what he'd do for you," Leigh said patting his shoulder. "When you want to know more, just ask."

Chad honked the horn and Patrick waved goodbye to his friend.

CHAPTER 13

BREAK SHOTS

The ring in Leigh's garage was considerably smaller than the ten-foot ones in the park. Patrick struggled with the lack of space to maneuver. A lawnmower, rakes, and shovels lined one side of the garage while the other contained bins and bins of holiday decorations. Bicycles and outdoor sports equipment filled a large area nearest the ring, so he had to squish himself into tight spaces to take a shot.

"Sorry, buddy," Leigh kept apologizing. "I'm just grateful I have this ring to practice on."

"Me, too," Patrick grunted.

Winter and snow arrived earlier than usual, which forced everyone inside more often. Curtis and Patrick had enjoyed bike riding together, but now even their bikes had been stored away. That left time for more practice sessions with Leigh.

"It's all about angle—the break shot—and how to line up your shooter," Leigh said, demonstrating. He sent his aggie spinning toward the third marble from the center of the ring, but at an angle so that it also lined up with the second marble on an adjacent row. He missed but knocked out a backup mib.

"Your turn," said Leigh.

"We're not playing a game, then?"

"No, Mrs. Lee wants us to practice break shots and all the distance shots one hundred times," Leigh answered.

"One hundred?" Patrick asked. He thought he might die. "Like at the park, hitting each tap shot ten times in a row?" He sighed.

"Ha, no." Leigh said. "She just suggested we do each type of shot one hundred times."

"All of them, today?"

"That's what she said," Leigh said, staring at Patrick.

"Can you set up a bed here in your garage for me because I know I'll pass out before we're finished," Patrick chortled.

Leigh laughed heartily.

Patrick discovered that he enjoyed lining up at certain angles to improve his break shot. He pictured himself playing pool and pretending his thumb was the cue stick. To prevent the monotony, he and Leigh told riddles and jokes until distance shots became the priority.

"A long shot, anywhere from about eighteen inches to the opposite side of the ring, takes concentration and patience," Leigh explained. "A crooked wrist, rolling your hand too far forward, and even a last second wiggle of your fingers will make you miss."

"Oh, great," Patrick grumbled.

"Think positively," Leigh reminded him. "Good attitude, remember?"

"How many different distance shots do we do?"

"How about four distances? Four hundred shots total for each of us," Leigh said taking a breath and letting it out slowly as he set a mib in the center of the circle, four feet away.

Both of them missed repeatedly until Patrick decided he'd had enough. As Leigh lined up to take a shot, Patrick aimed his shooter as if he intended to hit Leigh's agate. He flicked, and surprisingly that ugly, rough marble of his slammed into Leigh's aggie just as he released it.

"Whoa! That was awesome!" Leigh yelled. "I want to try."

Back and forth, they took aim at each other's shooters from across the ring, counting down to zero, they'd both flick and release. Occasionally the two shooters came together near the middle and smack! They cheered like witnessing a firework show.

"I'm counting this as distance practice," Patrick stated. "Besides, it's more fun!"

"True, but—oh, okay," Leigh said.

Weeks passed, and Patrick's callouses grew tougher. When Patrick showed up for practice, Leigh told him that they would be shooting 'ride-ins' and playing "shoot till you miss" games. "You get to start shooting from the middle of the ring with all thirteen marbles. Try to control your power and backspin so you can get a run of at least three marbles in a row or until you miss," Leigh explained.

"How do you know all these tricks? I mean games?" Patrick asked.

"Mrs. Lee taught me last summer when I prepared for nationals."

Patrick paused before he took aim and then sat back on his heels. "They call me Pudgy Knuckles at school."

"You don't like it?"

"They're making fun of my fat fingers!" Patrick whined. The day had been a rough one even though Ms. Hedgewick had been replaced with an elderly woman named Mrs. Belle, a long-term substitute. She treated everyone nicely, but it seemed to Patrick that she just wanted the year to end. So did he.

"You can look at it as teasing if you want, but who else gets a name like that?" Leigh said. "In marbles, it's kind of cool when you get a nickname. At nationals last year, some kids called a boy Mr. Stick."

"Why?" Patrick asked.

"If a person didn't know anything about marbles, they'd think his nickname had something to do with broken tree branches, but in marbles, it means that he is so good he can hit seven marbles in a row, a stick, consistently," Leigh said with a smile.

"Oh."

"I like your nickname," Leigh said sincerely.

"So, what are ride-ins?" inquired Patrick, not certain that he agreed with the nickname idea.

"Watch me." Leigh set a mib about six inches from the edge of the circle and aimed at it sideways.

"What're you doing? Why not just hit it straight on like a tap shot and make your shooter stick there? Your backspin works great!"

Leigh flicked his aggie sending it toward the side of the mib, and in turn, the mib rolled off to the side and out of the ring. "Look!" he said.

Patrick watched Leigh's shooter spin directly into the group of marbles set up in the middle. "I get it. Ride your shooter in so you can get closer to the rest of the mibs." When Patrick tried, he found it much more difficult than expected.

"The qualifying tournament is next month, Patrick. If we practice two days a week, I think you'll be ready."

Patrick agreed. However, the next day after school, when he informed Curtis that he intended to play marbles on Mondays, Wednesdays and Fridays, his friend dissented. "You're taking this marbles thing way too seriously, Patrick. We don't get to hang out as much," Curtis complained.

"I want to qualify for the national tournament," said Patrick.

"Can you? I mean that's a huge deal. Are you good enough?" Curtis drilled him.

"What? You think a pudgy kid like me can't do anything but play pranks?" Patrick responded sharply.

"Okay, show me, then!" Curtis demanded.

Patrick brushed some pebbles off the sidewalk. Pulling out his marbles sock, he flicked his shooter for backspin, and Curtis stared as it stuck there by Patrick's knees not rolling away. Then, he set up three tap shots, and after missing the first one, he thwacked three in a row. Finally, he stood up, pressed his fists into his hips, and glared at Curtis.

"Let me try," Curtis said. He imitated the flick of the thumb, but the shooter plopped to the ground. He tried again, and it zipped off into the grass. Setting a marble close to his hand, he squeezed the shooter; it rolled a bit barely touching the target mib. "Okay, so you've learned a lot, but are you going to go out there and win or make a fool of yourself?"

"You're jealous, Curtis!"

"I don't know anything about marbles, but I'm supposed to be your best friend, and you're spending more time with that middle school kid," shouted Curtis.

Sensing hurt and disappointment, Patrick realized that he had spent very little time with Curtis recently. In fact, his friend had no one else, just like him. Before marbles, they had only each other, and now Curtis felt left out.

"I'm sorry," Patrick said. "You're right."

With more restraint, Curtis said, "Well, then, what should we do about Carlos?"

"Uh, what about him?"

"He chases Gail at recess. You've seen him," Curtis said.

"Yeah, I'd like to smash him flat again."

"Me, too!" Curtis replied.

"Hmmm, I have an idea," Patrick said, grinning proudly.

With a little over a month of school left, they agreed it might have to be their last prank of fifth grade. Patrick wrote in disguised handwriting, "Dear Carlos, you're cute. XOXO."

"Make sure you always end it with 'love,'" Curtis suggested.

"Not yet. First, he'll wonder who wrote it, and then later she'll tell him she loves him," said Patrick. "You put it in his desk tomorrow."

Friday morning, Curtis slipped the love note to Carlos anonymously.

"Ooh, who's it from?" TJ asked looking around the room.

"I don't know," Carlos answered puzzled yet feeling pleased. "It's written in cursive."

"Start looking at girls' papers to find a match," said TJ, already engrossed in the love story.

Patrick smiled.

Twice a week for the next three weeks Patrick wrote mushier notes to Carlos, who was so bewildered by this girl's affection for him that he could hardly pay attention in class.

"I hope we can go to the movies on a date. I want you to kiss me if we do," said one of the notes. Carlos blushed so fiercely that even his lips turned red. He stuffed the note in his pocket and rushed to Ben and TJ.

"As soon as I find out who this is, I'm going to ask her to be my girlfriend," Carlos whispered within earshot of Curtis who immediately passed the news on to Patrick.

"Good, I'll write one last note," Patrick declared.

That night, he used a red pen and sketched hearts all around the words, "Oh Carlos, I've been waiting to tell you my name because I don't know if you like me or not. But I can't stand it anymore. You have to know it's me. I love you, Celia."

"If Celia finds out we did this, she'll kill us, you know," Curtis said on the way to school. "Then again, oh, well."

Carlos and his friends hung too close to his desk that morning, so Curtis passed the note to Patrick who waited until recess. Then he backtracked to the drinking fountain before he went out, giving him the perfect opportunity to set the note inside the desk.

As soon as Carlos read the letter, his eyes darted toward Celia who busied herself with her notebook and pencil before science class. Patrick no longer sat in the front row, so he was able to observe Carlos's reaction, tipping a nod at Curtis. *This is going to be good*, he thought.

And it was! Lunch recess set the stage for the most vehement display of young love to take place in elementary school. Carlos was surrounded by TJ, Ben, and a couple other boys who'd been given the inside scoop. He was prepared to make his move. Patrick and Curtis shifted shade trees to be within range of Celia, who sat at a picnic table with her friend.

"He's walking toward her," Curtis said, nudging Patrick. "He's talking to her. I wish we could hear better."

"You don't have to narrate. I'm seeing everything," Patrick stated.

Celia stood up to face Carlos, who wasted no time. He leaned in and placed a solid kiss on her mouth.

"Oh my gosh!" Patrick whooped in utter astonishment.

Celia shoved Carlos with all her strength and let out such a high-pitched scream that it sounded like a cat fighting to its death.

"What's wrong with you? You creep!" Celia screamed. "Your girlfriend? Yuck!" Curtis and Patrick heard her say.

Carlos staggered. Then he froze unable to move from total shock.

"And no! I don't love you!" Celia said. She stomped her foot and threw her hands in the air. "You warped excuse of a human being!" She raged on. "Don't ever touch me again!" Then she and her friend stormed away screaming insults at Carlos.

"Huh," Curtis said, flashing a rare look at Patrick. "And all this time, I thought she and Carlos would hit it off."

"I'm never going to forget this day for the rest of my life!" Patrick promised.

CHAPTER 14

QUALIFYING TOURNAMENT

Chad and Deedee set their lawn chairs close to the tournament rings. Curtis joined them. Other parents, relatives, and friends made themselves comfortable chatting with excitement. A newspaper reporter set up a tripod and camera. He grasped a notepad and pen in one hand.

Patrick felt sick to his stomach. "Ugh."

A handful of kids from competitive marbles club warmed up by taking practice shots on the rings. Patrick became suddenly aware of his size: baggy clown-like pants to cover his too large legs, blubbery arms from the shoulders to the wrists, a sagging mid-section. He felt extremely uncomfortable parading in front of the onlookers and reporter. He could already hear the whispers, "Have you ever seen someone so obese? How will he manage to get up and down? Who are his parents, are they fat too?"

"Pretend like it's just you and me in my garage," Leigh said. "Block everything else out. Remember, Pudgy Knuckles is a compliment to you as mibster," Leigh reassured him.

"Right," Patrick gulped. His hands were sweaty. He wiped them repeatedly on the rag Mrs. Lee had given him. "Fifty percent—I have to get an average of fifty percent to qualify," he mumbled.

Leigh gently spoke in his ear, "Positive attitude and good sportsmanship helps you play better."

Deedee kept twisting her fists in a circular motion. Chad finally held her hands. "Honey, relax." He waved at Patrick who stood with the rest of the competitors waiting for game matchups.

"Patrick and Cory, ring one," Mrs. Lee called. Patrick heard nothing else after that.

Cory won the lag and set the rack up. Just before he took aim, Patrick remembered they hadn't shaken hands yet, so he interrupted the shot and reached out his hand.

"Oh yeah," Cory said. "I'm nervous. I forgot."

Patrick sighed in relief. He wasn't alone.

Cory won the first game, and Patrick won the break for the next game. He envisioned Leigh's garage, and selected an angle. He took a practice flick for spin then aimed. His black shooter sped toward a line of marbles scattering them in an array. He managed to send one target marble as well as his shooter out of the ring. After a few shaky innings, the game was tied. Patrick needed one mib to win. Nothing was left but long shots. He pretended that Leigh crouched opposite him with his aggie.

In his mind Patrick counted down, *Three, two, one, zero.* He spun his marble toward a distant mib hitting it dead on and won the game.

The sun shone directly overhead, and the temperature rose. The audience fanned themselves or moved to shadier areas to watch the final games, one of which matched up Leigh and Patrick. Up to this point, Leigh was undefeated and shooting excellently. He even played two perfect games, getting sticks before his opponent even had a chance to shoot. Patrick felt like a *stick* of melting butter. His rag was soaked already.

Leigh took the initiative and shook Patrick's hand encouraging him to play his best, while Patrick could think of nothing else except, "I hope you get another stick!"

Leigh won the lag but missed his first shot.

"You did that on purpose, Leigh," Patrick whispered. "Don't let me win because you feel sorry for me."

"If I let you win, then I'd be a poor sport and you wouldn't *earn* your way to nationals," Leigh reminded him. "I honestly missed that shot."

Curtis squatted near their ring, silently hoping that Patrick would win both games, and Leigh would step out of his best friend's life.

Patrick aimed, knocked out a mib, and his shooter remained spinning in the center with the twelve mibs still in place. His tap shots had improved tremendously since he and Leigh practiced them so much, so he squeezed his shooter and flicked lightly sending another mib out of the ring. Still close to a set of marbles, he flicked again earning dubs. His shooter rolled out, however.

"Wow!" Leigh clapped Patrick's back. "Amazing and well done." Then, Leigh managed to score a total of two on his next turn.

Surprisingly, the game was tied five to five at the end of five innings with only one turn left for each. Leigh attempted a ride-in hoping to count it and then hit the seventh marble out to win, but he only brushed the mib scoring nothing. Patrick also missed leaving the game to be decided by a lag. Whoever won the lag, won the game.

Deedee stood up. "Go Pattycake!" she hollered.

Some people snickered. Patrick was mortified.

Leigh leaned near him and whispered, "Pudgy Knuckles, you're a star!"

"One, two, three, lag," the referee called out.

The two shooters rolled closer and closer to the lag line and were seemingly tied. The referee bent over keeping her eye on them. "Don't move," she told the boys, "until they stop." She eyed them and then called Mrs. Lee over. "It's too close to call. You need to measure."

Deedee stepped as near to the ring as allowed with her hands clasped like she was praying. Patrick sweated with anxiety, and Mrs. Lee carefully laid the ruler down, measuring the exact distance the edge of each shooter lay to the line.

"One-half inch in difference!" Mrs. Lee announced. "Superb lags, young men. However, the winner is Patrick!"

Deedee squealed and other people clapped as the lag had drawn attention to onlookers. Leigh shook Patrick's pudgy knuckles and said, "You broke my winning streak. Well done. It keeps me humble." Leigh smiled broadly.

The tournament concluded a while later to Patrick's relief. He hunkered down under a shade tree and waited for the results. Curtis settled down next to him. A few other parents congratulated him for playing well. The crowd buzzed with anticipation. The newspaper reporter prepared for interviews and photos of the winners.

Mrs. Lee held the names of the champions in her hand. She congratulated every participant and encouraged them to continue to play marbles even if they didn't qualify today. The trophies she set out were impressive: two glittering blue and sapphire columns attached to white marble bases with golden cups on top. Patrick knew in his heart that Leigh qualified. He wondered about himself since he'd won some games and scored quite a few points. He just hoped it reached fifty percent.

Patrick knew that Mrs. Lee could take two boys and two girls to the national tournament if they qualified. Even if they shot well, she insisted they had to be good sports or she wouldn't take them. So as she called the best sports to the center ring, a shy girl of about thirteen-years-old named Lissy, nervously accepted her award. A young boy, new to competitive marbles, also received the award. She asked them to remain standing as she called the place winners to the ring.

"In first place for the girls, with a score of fifty-one marbles and sixty percent, is Lissy! I'd also like to say that she has qualified to compete at the national tournament!" Mrs. Lee announced the second-place girl, who didn't qualify. "And first place for the boys is Leigh with a score of sixty marbles and seventy-one percent, also a qualifier for nationals!"

Patrick wobbled from anxiety. He grabbed his dad's shoulder and took a long breath. "Please, oh, please be me," he mumbled softly.

"Finally, our second-place winner is Patrick with thirty-nine marbles and forty-six percent." She paused and locked her eyes on Patrick, who stood motionless, his face pale and eyes tearing up.

Forty-six isn't enough, he thought. He was devastated.

Mrs. Lee resumed, "Patrick please join us up here on the ring. I've decided to invite you to the national marbles tournament!"

Patrick could hardly move as his knees buckled, and he stumbled forward. Immediately, Curtis drew Patrick's arm over his shoulder to help him up, but of course, he was a load of dead weight. Chad grabbed his son's hand, pulling him up and gently shoving him ahead.

"Go, Patrick," he said proudly. "You're going to Wildwood, New Jersey!"

Strangers cheered him on, clapping enthusiastically. Eventually, he slid next to Leigh to receive his trophy. Suddenly people snapped photos and congratulated them loudly. There was a reporter and a camera broadcasting the action. He pulled Patrick aside.

"What made you decide to shoot marbles?" the reporter asked.

"I—uh, my fourth grade teacher invited me to the club."

"How much do you practice?" he questioned.

"About six hours a week, I think," replied Patrick nervously.

"What do you expect at the national competition?"

"Well, I don't know." He hadn't considered that. "It will be hard, I guess."

"Do you have a special shooter that you'll take with you?" he asked. He stopped writing, waiting to check out the marble.

Patrick was overwhelmed and couldn't answer. Leigh overheard the reporter and came closer to give input. "He just earned his first agate, which our coach will fit him with today."

The reporter turned his attention to Leigh and began questioning him about his return to nationals, his agate, who he wanted to thank, and so on.

Next, Mrs. Lee gathered her national competitors and their families together for a serious discussion. Curtis included himself. "Champions," she said, "Going to Wildwood for a week of marbles is the ultimate adventure of a lifetime."

"That's true," Leigh piped in.

"You represent your families, your team, your county, and your state, and I insist on the highest level of sportsmanship in my players. I promise you that the competition will be tough, and that's why I set a fifty-percent accuracy threshold." She raised her hand to Patrick, but he didn't know what to do.

"I only shot at forty-six percent," Patrick said timidly.

"Yes, Patrick, but you played with one-hundred percent good attitude! And I believe that by the time we leave in six weeks, you'll meet the higher goal."

He beamed.

"We have a great deal of preparations to make and a very short time to do so. Therefore," Mrs. Lee said, "I need a commitment from you and your families." She went on to describe costs and fundraising, travel commitments—at least one parent must accompany the player—and a strenuous practice schedule.

"Patrick and Lissy, today you have earned your very own agate shooter. They're tough to come by, at least the good ones are, so I reserve them for national competitors only." She opened a box with several tiny, zippered bags, each one holding an agate. They drew near gaping at the beauties.

"Can I see too?" Curtis asked, pushing in between them.

Mrs. Lee fitted Lissy first, selecting a shooter that fit perfectly in her petite hands yet was still legal size, and she managed to spin it nicely. A seventh grader, like Leigh, she had only participated in competitive club, and even though Patrick had played some games against her, he hardly knew her. Then Mrs. Lee examined Patrick's fingers quite fastidiously and set three shooters in front of him. "With your power, Patrick, you need a larger marble, but since your spin is also coming along, a smaller marble would also suit you. See what you think," she said.

Curtis grabbed them first as if he felt obligated to see to it that his best friend chose the winning marble, but Patrick simply asked to see the dark brown one first. Squeezing it tightly between his thumb and index finger, it felt similar to his black glass one. He flicked and it spun; he shot, and it rolled evenly. Then, he selected a smaller white, layered one, and it too obeyed his fingers. Finally, he picked up a reddish one with a black spot on it thinking it resembled the planet Mars.

"This one is awesome!" he stated, already wanting it.

"Yes, it's a rarer agate, pretty, and worth more," Mrs. Lee agreed. "Test it, though."

He flicked it and shot with power, but the Mars marble rolled straight at first, then wobbled unsteadily as it slowed. He tried again, and it veered in one direction. "Why is it doing that?" Patrick inquired.

"May I try?" Leigh asked.

Leigh flicked with amazing backspin, and the shooter spun in one spot but vibrated unusually. He inspected it. "It's not completely round," he decided, handing it to Mrs. Lee.

"It has a minor indent, but the mibster has to choose, though."

Patrick examined it again. He desperately wanted it, but Curtis shook his head.

"Humph," Patrick grumbled, spinning the brown marble again and finally selecting it. "It's pretty too," he said.

"Ha," Leigh laughed. "It won't be after we rough it up."

CHAPTER 15
WILDWOOD DAYS

Curtis joined Patrick for every practice in preparation for the National Marbles Tournament, proving to be the best fan club ever. He cheered him on, handed him water and snacks, and learned the ways of Ringer like a mibster. Also, Patrick's dad and mom purchased knee pads and wrist and forehead sweatbands. Mrs. Lee had even provided the entire entourage with team shirts.

Deedee proudly told all her friends that Pattycake was a real athlete now. Two evenings before their departure, she held a surprise party to wish him both a successful trip and tournament. Unfortunately, Chad had to stay home and work. Patrick secretly cried when he found out he couldn't join them.

"Pack this way," Deedee said rearranging his suitcase. "And yes, you're taking this new swimming suit."

Patrick found it useless to argue as she had taken charge of every detail imaginable. He made it his purpose to keep his marbles safe and his nerves from overtaking him. He'd never flown before and feared the plane would crash. He'd never seen the ocean. And above all, he couldn't believe for the life of him that he, Fatsy Patsy the cow, was competing in a national tournament.

Curtis and his dad met them at the airport for the farewell, and to Patrick's surprise, Curtis choked up as he hugged him. "I'll see you when you get back. I have a new bike trail to ride and," he lowered his voice to a whisper, "I thought up the greatest bubble gum prank ever!"

"Call me every night," Chad told Deedee and Patrick. "I want all the news." He embraced them and then through security they embarked.

Patrick decided the plane ride couldn't be worse than airport security—they literally searched him and his pockets. What humiliation! Finally, boarding the aircraft and taking a window seat, he peered through the tiny frame wondering if he'd ever see his dad and Curtis again.

His mom patted his leg. "Don't worry," she said, "you'll enjoy this new experience." She smoothed her pants, fluffed her hair, and painted her lips for departure.

Patrick held on. The airplane shook and rattled at take-off, but soon the vibration and hum put him to sleep.

They landed a while later. "Hurry up, Pattycake! We need to switch flights," his mom said making him rush through the airport to a new terminal.

"Mom, I'm exhausted and my head feels fuzzy," Patrick complained. They made their next flight, and once again, Patrick feared the take-off.

Finally, they arrived in Philadelphia.

Mrs. Lee and Mr. Jerry had arrived earlier and waited for them, so they could all ride together. Deedee expressed her gratitude as she feared driving in unknown territory. Soon, the group headed south through New Jersey and on to Wildwood. Patrick observed nothing but trees for miles and miles.

"Where're the hills and the beach? Why so many trees?" he asked.

"We're a long way from Colorado," Mr. Jerry replied. "And very soon, the trees will wane, and the coast will appear.

Sure enough, the end of the world quickly approached as Patrick gazed out the window seeing a string of hotels along what must be the ocean. Wildwood lay just ahead. Rolling the window down, a rush of salty air filled the car along with a sensation he'd never felt.

"The air is sticky," Patrick said, rubbing his arm.

"It's humid," his mother said. "I look forward to moist air on my skin and hair. What a person wouldn't do to have such a thing as humidity facial products. Aw," she hummed.

"Look, Patrick," Mrs. Lee said, pointing toward the Wildwood boardwalk entry with giant, decorative beach balls. "To our left, an old hotel called The Rio used to fill this space welcoming all the mibsters to the national tournament. It's since been torn down, and we stay at a different hotel closer to Ringer Stadium now."

Patrick soaked in the scenery feeling completely lost yet thrilled beyond imagination.

"The Beach Terrace Motor Inn. We're here," Mr. Jerry announced, already recognizing people loitering in the parking lot.

Mrs. Lee rolled her window down to say hello to an old friend, then parked in the shade of the building. "Time to check in and receive room assignments." Deedee pulled out her hand mirror, double-checked her face, then put on a smile. Patrick stayed close to Mrs. Lee who hugged every other person they came in contact with, then led them to a table where official people greeted them.

"I'd like to introduce a new player this year, Patrick Melberry," Mrs. Lee said.

One of the gentlemen shook his hand and nodded at Deedee. "You're already a champion just by earning your right to be here," the guy said, grinning widely.

"Oh, thanks," Patrick said, shyly.

Settling into their room on the fifth floor, Deedee began to unpack while Patrick stepped out onto the balcony taking in the spectacular view of a water park and an enormous Ferris wheel. Off in the distance, the ocean surf pounded the shore. Three decks below, kids splashed in a pool.

"Patrick!" Alejandro waved at him from his balcony two rooms away. "My sister and I both qualified this year! I can't wait!"

"Hey," Patrick shouted gleefully. "I'll come to your balcony."

The two boys chattered incessantly about the week, the schedule, and the other mibsters they had yet to meet as seagulls squawked noisily overhead. Already, butterflies bounced off the inside of Patrick's stomach as he anticipated the tournament. Rosia, Alejandro's eight-year-old sister, jumped on her bed singing silly songs. "She barely qualified," Alejandro said. "Mr. Jerry thinks she'll do okay in the tournament, though."

"I'm nervous," Patrick admitted.

"Me, too, but we're part of the Colorado team. Mr. Jerry says we all need to support each other."

"Yeah."

Before long, Patrick's mom called him to the room to prepare for the evening banquet. "Dress nicely, Pattycake," she told him. She wore a fashionable sundress and matching flowers in her hair.

Patrick cringed at the crisp, cotton dress shirt and shorts she'd purchased for the occasion. "They're scratchy. And Mom, I'm not used to wearing short pants."

"We're at the beach," she said matter-of-factly. "People wear clothes like these here."

"Ugh!"

Mrs. Lee met them at the banquet hall along with the entire Colorado group, who managed to find seats together at one long table. At the opposite end, a team from Tennessee were engaged in a giggly conversation. Patrick assumed they were making fun of him. He felt uncomfortable in his clothes and uncertain if he would be welcomed here.

An announcer introduced the committee, then gave a short

speech as a slide show of past champions scrolled across the television screens. Then Mr. Jerry stepped up to the podium and prayed over the mibsters and the meal. Delicious plates of food and plenty of soda spread out from one end of each table to the other. The hall's atmosphere was full of energy and excitement. However, Patrick could hardly eat for the first time in his life.

"Don't pick at your meal, Pattycake. Are you sick?" his mom asked. "Do we need to go to the room? I'm worried about you." She'd turned into a mother hen all of a sudden, frantically fussing about food.

"Mrs. Melberry," Mrs. Lee said, "He'll start eating once the jitters calm down. Look around, he's not the only one with a bucket of nerves on their plates."

"Oh—oh I see," Deedee replied. "Okay."

Before dinner ended, the committee made their way to the podium where they announced each mibster by name, requesting they come to the stage to receive their tournament shirts and swag bag. Midway through the banquet, each member of the Colorado team was called.

"Patrick Melberry," the guy with the microphone said.

"I can't do this," Patrick whispered to Leigh. "People will laugh at my fat!"

"You're more than what you look like," Leigh responded. "Go get your shirt!"

Airport security was a piece of cake compared to this, he thought as he slogged across the stage.

Later, as the sun set, the boardwalk burst into life and lights. Amusement park rides blinked in beautiful patterns to attract riders. Music blared, and Patrick couldn't sleep. Tomorrow morning the tournament would commence, and he felt out of place, like he didn't belong. "How did I get myself into this?" he groaned.

A salty breeze blew through Ringer Stadium; ten official marble pads embedded in the sand next to the boardwalk, sets of bleachers, a covered stage, banners, and a wooden sign declaring it the home of the national tournament. Droves of mibsters and their friends and families erected canopies. Mrs. Lee placed her beach tent near the stage where a stronger breeze blew. Leigh sat inside flicking his aggie into his palm.

"Hi, Patrick! Dump your stuff in here. Where's your mom?"

"She's coming," Patrick said, dropping his tournament bag. He wore his sweatbands and knee pads and proceeded to cover his bare arms, legs, and face with sunscreen.

"No!" Leigh shouted. "Don't get it on your hands. Your shooter will slip out every time."

"Then how? All I have is lotion."

"Use my spray instead."

The committee tested the speakers and addressed the crowd and the onlookers gathering on the boardwalk. Referees picked up their clipboards and brooms and headed to their respective rings. The announcer yelled with enthusiasm, "Knuckles down! Let the games begin!"

"I have to go to the bathroom!" Patrick said, panicking. "Where is it?"

"Right now!?" Leigh asked. "Uh, it's over there at that restaurant or down half a block, that way. They're starting to call names."

"I know, but I can't wait. I can't!"

Just then, Leigh's name sounded over the speaker, and he jumped up, leaving Patrick in a tizzy.

He searched madly for a place to pee, knowing he'd never make it to the nearest restrooms in time. "Oh no!" He started toward the restaurant his bladder about to burst. Terrified that he'd have an accident on the spot, he waddled under the boardwalk, looked both ways, and let go! Rattling bike tires sounded overhead. Thinking he'd escaped detection, he sighed.

"Patrick Melberry!" his mother screeched in horror as she ducked under a low part of the boardwalk, tiptoeing through the moist sand toward the bleachers.

He spun, still in action, spraying the ground in a semicircle. "Mom!"

The first day of the National Marbles Tournament had begun. What a way for it to start! Patrick bowed his head, slumped dejectedly away from his mom and dropped heavily onto the beach tent floor. Sand stuck to every inch of his bared skin, and his fingers felt like sandpaper.

"Patrick Melberry!" the guy with the microphone called out. "You're needed on ring ten for a match."

A tall man with the most unique moustache and wearing a straw hat with dangles pouring over the rim waved a clipboard at him. Another boy, his opponent, stood patiently on the wooden edge of the platform. Patrick clambered onto the ring and pulled his agate out of his pocket.

"Shake the sand off your feet before you step up from now on," the referee said. Then he picked up a straw broom with colorful pompoms attached to it and swept the new sand to a corner. "I'm the Marble Man," he said smiling. "Ready to play a great game?"

The other boy nodded. They shook hands. Patrick forgot to look into his eyes and give encouragement. Unaware of anything but anxious fear, he lost the lag and watched his opponent score four marbles on his first turn. Patrick missed altogether. The game ended the second inning with the boy winning seven to zero. Patrick took the break in the next game knocking one mib out, but his shooter bounced wildly off the platform and into the sand. After a brief search, the game resumed, and the boy from Pittsburg stuck him, that is, got a stick, which concluded the match.

The Marble Man stopped Patrick from leaving the ring.

"Remember that you're a champion. Every kid here, no matter how old he is or how long he's been playing, has earned the right to participate today. Someone will win this entire tournament, and all the rest will consider themselves losers unless they believe in who they are and practice good sportsmanship." He paused. "I believe in you, young man."

Patrick seemed to snap out of a trance and start breathing again. He looked up at the gentleman and smiled. "Thanks, I needed to hear that." Then he shook the referee's hand and thanked him again. After that, Patrick tried to engage in each game and, win or lose, give compliments. Unfortunately, he lost quite a few.

A photographer showed up midmorning for the flag ceremony and group picture. Last year's boy and girl champion raised the American flag to its highest point on the pole as boardwalk speakers boomed out the national anthem. Next, every mibster in his or her white tournament shirt sat, kneeled, or stood for photos.

A catchy tune played loudly as boardwalk spectators and many mibsters and referees began dancing and singing despite the fact that matches had resumed. "Wild Wildwood days, oh baby, every day's a holiday and every night is a Saturday night. Oh, those Wildwood days, wild, wild Wildwood days." Patrick was simply amused.

Not long after that, a strange train car of some type navigated along a path on the boardwalk repeating an obnoxious warning "Wa—wa—watch the tramcar, please!" Rollercoasters squeaked as riders screamed, while boardwalk shops and carnival booths opened, making it exceptionally difficult to focus on the marbles games. The humidity made the rising temperatures more sweltering, and Patrick perspired uncontrollably. Besides that, sand had made its way into the folds of his knee pads causing painful rubbing, so he removed them.

"Pattycake, you need them for your knees, and they give you an athletic look," she told him.

"Mom, I'm dying out here. I don't care whether I look athletic or not!" He kicked off his shoes as well and tromped through the sand in his bare feet like some of the other mibsters.

"There may be glass in the sand," he heard her say as he stepped onto a ring for his next match.

Hot, exhausted and hurting, he joined Leigh and Lissy at the tent. They also appeared worn out. Lissy had completed her matches for the day and seemed content with how she fared. Leigh, on the other hand, had struggled against his powerful opponents who managed to stick him twice.

For Patrick's last game of the day, the referee thought that his opponent's shooter was too large and asked for a gauge. A committee member strolled to the ring holding a shiny device with two holes in it. Below one hole was the word *Go*, and below the other hole were the words *No Go*. The boy dropped his agate through the Go hole, and it wouldn't pass through. The kid started to argue and complain, but the guy with the gauge said, "This tool was designed by an employee of NASA who saw to it that it was accurate."

"NASA? Really?" Patrick asked.

"Take a look. It has the official N.I.S.T. mark on it, which ensures that the measurements are exact," he answered. "Here's NASA's symbol too! And to make this more special it was created as the National Marbles Tournament's official gauge. It was even launched into space!"

Patrick stared at it. "Incredible!" He asked to touch it, then felt a final surge of energy to complete his last game.

Finally, day one of preliminaries ended and families headed to their rooms, the beach, or the pool. Deedee couldn't bear to spend another minute in the sun, so she left Patrick to his own devices. It took Leigh and Alejandro a tremendous amount of persuading to get Patrick in a swimsuit and into the pool, where a few kids tossed a ball to each other. Rather than step into the shallow end they convinced him to cannonball it, so Patrick balled up and bounded into the water creating an enormous splash. The children all cheered. Tired as he was, the water was refreshing, and the other kids welcomed him and his teammates to their ball game.

CHAPTER 16

TOURING THE ISLAND

"Boat ride, boat ride, boat ride," the announcer kept saying. Mibsters launched into day two of preliminaries, and Patrick felt less nervous, so much so that he was able to eat half a dozen donuts for breakfast. Now, he stood on a ring, waiting for his opponent to tape his blistered finger.

"What's the boat ride?" Patrick asked the referee.

"Oh," she said, "a chartered boat takes people out onto the ocean to watch dolphins. If you want to go, just have your parent buy tickets at the stage."

A boy from Ohio stepped onto the ring, apologized, and prepared for the lag. When Patrick shook his hand he said, "Don't let that blister get in your way. You're going to play well."

The boy smiled. "Thanks," he said.

They split the match one game each. Patrick dug his toes into the warm sand as he crossed over to Mrs. Lee's tent. Rosia giggled as Lissy told her about her last game. Apparently, a cute boy stared at Lissy's opponent throughout, completely distracting her.

"I don't like boys," Rosia stated. "Except for you, Patrick, because you're nice to me."

"Uh, okay," Patrick said, shrugging his shoulders.

Mrs. Lee volunteered to referee all day, and Mr. Jerry leaned against the stage talking with someone. "Our marbles program in Colorado works incredibly hard to raise money to attend nationals. Without our sponsors, we wouldn't be able to afford it."

"Hi, Mr. Jerry," Patrick said.

"Hello, Patrick." Mr. Jerry said. "I'd like for you to meet someone. Patrick is one of our mibsters. He's a good sport."

"Hi, Patrick. I'm happy to meet you. My name is Rick Mawhinney from Cumberland, Maryland." He shook Patrick's hand. "What do you think of Wildwood and the tournament?"

"I can't really believe I'm here," Patrick answered.

Rick grinned. "Are you joining us on the boat ride this afternoon?"

"I hope so," Patrick answered.

Mr. Mawhinney left them to speak to one of the scorekeepers, his daughter, in fact.

"He's a national champion, Patrick," Mr. Jerry said.

"What!? Wow!" Patrick's eyes grew wide. "I shook the hand of a champion?"

"There's quite a few past champions here," he explained as he pointed out several of the referees, a woman in a beach chair with an umbrella, a bearded man leaning over the railing on the boardwalk, a guy and girl sitting on the bleachers, and at least one of the scorekeepers.

"No kidding?" Patrick asked. He was astonished and felt kind of important to be in their midst.

Leigh appeared tons happier today and had won most of his games. "Do you have boat ride tickets yet?" he asked Patrick.

"I'm asking my mom now," Patrick answered.

His mom was fanning herself on a bleacher. Behind her on the boardwalk a seagull had snatched a piece of pizza from a girl, and it had fallen to the sand below. What emerged was a whirlwind of birds, shrieking and flapping their wings fighting for the pizza. Everyone on the bleacher except for Deedee scattered.

"What happened? Why did everyone just freak out?" Deedee asked as Patrick approached. Then it hit her—literally. In the chaos, a seagull flew over her head and released a stream of poop into her beautiful hair. She screamed. In a crazed state of shock, she jumped down from the bleacher and immediately darted back to the hotel.

Darn, I wanted to ride the boat, Patrick thought. As he was returning to the tent, he noticed that Mr. Jerry was standing in line to buy tickets, so he explained to him what had happened. Mr. Jerry kindly bought boat ride tickets for him and his mom.

A bit later, the announcer called both Patrick and Leigh to ring one where the previous year's boy champion refereed. Only fourteen-years-old, the three boys cracked jokes during the match making it seem like back home. At any rate, Leigh beat Patrick both games, and they hugged rather than shook hands. Immediately after their game, Patrick and Alejandro met up for a match.

"I just got a stick!" Alejandro announced proudly. "I'm on a roll."

Somehow that dampened Patrick's spirits and shrunk his confidence. He tried, but Alejandro won both games as well, leaving him with four wins and ten losses for day two. Happy the competition ended for the day, he looked forward to a boat ride.

"Will the seagulls fly over the boat?" Deedee asked.

"I don't know, Mom," Patrick answered.

As everyone climbed aboard, the whole Colorado team ventured to the top deck, except for Deedee, who sat protected under cover below. The sun's rays danced across the water, and Patrick was in awe of the expanse. Sensing the rocking motion as the captain guided the boat into deeper waters, he felt a bit nauseous.

Mrs. Lee recognized Patrick's distress and handed him a ginger ale, which took the edge off. Before long, dolphins appeared behind the boat, gliding in the wake. Everyone hooted or exclaimed their joy, especially Patrick.

"I can't believe how gigantic they are!"

"Whales are bigger," a boy about Patrick's age commented. "Hi, I'm Troy from Tennessee. We haven't played each other yet."

"We play tomorrow, the last day of preliminaries?" Patrick said. "This is my first year."

"Mine too. I'm not winning very much, but it's still fun," Troy said.

The two boys connected quickly, discovering they both had a knack for pranks. And marbles. They promised to keep in touch and work hard to come back again next year. The captain pointed out a place called Cape May, Wildwood Crest, and quite a few different docked fishing boats they passed.

"What's that floating object down there?" Patrick asked.

"A horseshoe crab," Mr. Jerry said. We'll take a trip to Cape May tomorrow, and you'll see more of them."

As the boat ride came to an end, Troy and Patrick planned to hang out by the pool that evening and play cards and drink soda. Leigh and Alejandro wanted to join them. After dinner, they all had a good time hanging out.

After getting ready for bed, Patrick entered his mom's room. "You know what, Mom?" He caught her attention. "The kids here like me."

"Oh, Pattycake, they're all just being polite to you."

"Really, Mom?" Patrick asked. He was aggravated. "You think people can't like me because I'm fat!"

"They don't want to hurt your feelings, and of course they could like you. I know you're heavy, but I love you," his mom stammered.

"I'm worth more than my weight!" Patrick retorted. He crawled in his bed, picturing himself as a hovering drone recapturing the day's events. He fell asleep believing that he'd been accepted by the other mibsters.

Day three of preliminaries proved to be intense. The best shooters vied for the top eight places in order to make semifinals. Alejandro and Leigh held eighth and ninth places respectively after two days. Patrick sat in sixteenth place while Lissy and Rosia came out somewhere in the middle of the girls' league.

Patrick played fairly well his first few matches, and then felt a little sick from the heat. His skin soaked up a little too much sun on the boat ride, so it had turned a rosy red making him quite uncomfortable. The lack for a breeze didn't help. Mrs. Lee had encouraged them to drink a lot of water and use a cooling rag, but Deedee purchased Patrick a large caramel frappé to comfort and cool him off. His coach frowned, then filled in for a referee needing a break.

With only a few more matches to play, Patrick started to falter, as did some other mibsters. The committee kept the games rolling, but it was rough. The day dragged, but eventually preliminaries were over. Before the semi-finalists were announced, however, the former champions geared up for their tournament: a single elimination bracket playing to seven marbles. Patrick feared it would take forever, yet to his surprise, several won with immediate sticks. Rick Mawhinney made it to the finals match against a girl who had won two years earlier. She lost the lag, and he beat her two games in a row.

Despite heat exhaustion, Patrick was astounded by the quality of their shooting. He congratulated Mr. Mawhinney and then joined the crowd facing the stage. Deedee came down from her perch on the bleachers and stood in the heat with other parents.

The committee speeded up the announcement due to the hot

and humid weather. In no particular order, they read off all eight girls' names. Lissy and Rosia hadn't made the cut, but they already knew they wouldn't. Patrick wondered and worried about Leigh's spot. As they called the names, the boy from Pittsburgh, who beat Patrick his first match, ran to the stage followed by a boy from Tennessee, then Alejandro.

One spot remained. Patrick glanced at Leigh, who seemed to be praying. Finally, they called him up to join the other seven semifinalists. Patrick breathed a sigh of relief. The audience clapped, took some photos, then dispersed quickly.

Back in the cool comfort of his room, Patrick napped peacefully until Mr. Jerry knocked on the door. "Time to leave for Cape May," he said.

Driving to the tip of New Jersey didn't take long. When they got to the lighthouse, the scenery had changed. Lush greenery spread out around them, and the area wasn't bustling with boardwalk enthusiasts. Deedee preferred this place.

"One hundred ninety-nine steps to the top," Mr. Jerry said, pointing up. In great condition, he began the ascent while Deedee and Patrick trailed behind.

"I've climbed this many times," Mrs. Lee said, catching up. "It's worth it."

Patrick huffed and puffed, stopping every few steps on the spiral, iron staircase.

"Pattycake, you don't have to do this if it's too hard," Deedee said. "You can wait for us at the bottom."

"Yes, he does!" Mrs. Lee stated. "This rare experience needs to be part of his national tournament adventure."

"Humph," Deedee grumbled, continuing to climb.

"I'll stay with you, Patrick," said Mrs. Lee.

"I *do* want to make it," he said, pushing himself to continue.

Ultimately, they circled the outdoor balcony, soaking in the view from the top. The gorgeous barrier island landscape in connection with the greenish silver sea filled Patrick's heart with a sense of peace. A soft breeze brushed his face and hair while shore-birds soared in the sky.

"I love it up here!" he told his mom. "I knew I could make it."

Mr. Jerry declared that if they were to make their reservation at the seafood restaurant, they'd better hustle. The quaint, Victorian town of Cape May intrigued Patrick. He admired the beautiful, coastal buildings, thinking one day he'd like to spend more time there.

"Oh, what's that smell?" Patrick asked.

"Fresh seafood," Mr. Jerry said. "Right from the ocean to the table."

They were seated in the open-air restaurant. Patrick scanned the menu, screwing up his face at the odd selection of shellfish. He finally settled on a hamburger and fries.

"Pattycake, you can't order food like that at an authentic seafood restaurant. Try some scallops or oysters."

"I want a hamburger. It's on the menu."

"It's fine," Mrs. Lee said. I'll order seafood that Patrick can taste."

He nibbled at lobster, crab, and scallops that turned his taste buds upside down, then he gobbled up what he ordered. He felt better for it, too, partly because he wasn't fond of the seafood, but also because Mrs. Lee stood up for him twice that day so far.

Following dinner, Mr. Jerry drove down a dead-end lane and parked.

"Where are we now?" asked Patrick.

"Sunset Beach, where, you guessed it, we'll watch the sun set," he answered.

The pebbles on this beach felt nothing like the sands of Wild-wood. They poked at the arches of his feet and stuck between his toes. Patrick bent over to remove them and discovered nearly clear stones as smooth as ice cubes and resembling diamonds. He gath-ered several of them, then ventured toward the ocean that lapped against what appeared to be a black, volcanic rock.

A stranger wearing a US military cap stepped near Patrick. Pointing at the remains of a ship not far from shore, he said, "In World War One, a company designed and built concrete ships. That one ran aground, and its skeleton has been sinking ever since."

"Really?" Patrick pondered. "Concrete?"

The man nodded, then moseyed along.

A group of people crowded around something washed ashore, so Patrick went to investigate. Mrs. Lee also seemed interested. A horseshoe crab lay in the pebbles. No one touched it. A bit of Curtis washed over Patrick, and he fearlessly grasped the outer shell of the animal, picking it up with its many segmented legs wiggling desperately. Surprised that it was alive, he extended his arms as its sharp, spiny tail flashed this way and that like a sword.

"Oh, my!" Deedee cried in alarm.

People squealed with delight as Patrick became the center of attention. They snapped photos while he smiled proudly. Then, he decided to release it in the water, so he marched to the water's edge. Never having set foot in the ocean, he had trouble setting the horseshoe crab in the receding waves more than once; it kept washing back.

I'm going to do this, he said to himself. Lifting the struggling animal to shoulder height, Patrick waded waist deep into the water sensing the power of the undertow pulling at his ankles.

"Patrick, your clothes. Stop! It's not safe!" Patrick's mother exclaimed, fretting loudly. Patrick felt strong for the first time in his life. Perhaps all of the up and down exercise he received from playing hundreds of marbles games, toughened his muscles. *Or maybe*, he thought, *I'm more than just a fat kid*. Patrick set the animal on its belly, and at once it swam out to sea.

Patrick grinned mischievously. He ducked under a swell, tasted the salty water, sensed it swirling his hair, then jumped up feeling light and buoyant. Again and again, he found great pleasure in the experience, realizing that some part of who he used to be had vanished.

Having had the best time of his life, he crouched on the shore, listening to a scratchy song about patriotism pour from a beach speaker and counting the seconds until the blood red sun drifted under the horizon. His heart was aglow.

CHAPTER 17

TRAGEDY STRIKES

The Wildwood days were coming to a close. Patrick gathered around the championship ring with all his friends on the last day of the tournament. Neither Leigh nor Alejandro made it to finals, yet they gave it their all in the semis, finishing in sixth and seventh place respectively. Each shot of the boys' finals was announced over loudspeakers. Silence felt eerie as they lined up for breaks, ride-ins, and seventh marble shots. He observed their acute concentration, thinking what it would be like if he were in their place. Anxiety suddenly flooded over him.

"The game marble and championship shot," the announcer commented observing the final flick that ended the tournament.

The winner was swarmed by friends, family, reporters. Patrick stood up to let the revelry onto the ring. He cheered as well, feeling warmth and friendship, and more than anything, a sense of belonging.

Later that evening, a dedication to the previous year's champions was held at the National Marbles Hall of Fame. Patrick listened, yet fidgeted because his mind was set on amusement park rides yet to come. Finally, the ceremony ended, and he and a sizeable group of mibsters hit the boardwalk. Three piers of the most impressive thrill-seeking rides awaited them. And they screamed as the rollercoasters sped them swiftly down the tracks and spun them upside down. They cried out in playful fear making their way through a haunted ship. They soared among the stars on the enormous Ferris wheel. Tired and dizzy, the group took a break and munched on funnel cakes shrouded in sugar and recollected the fun times they'd shared during that wonderful week in Wildwood.

Chad wrapped his welcoming arms around Patrick and Deedee as they debarked the plane. After they told him the tournament results, he begged for stories, so they chattered unceasingly all the way home. Patrick couldn't wait to see Curtis and tell him everything, but his parents made him unpack first. Then he rushed to his best friend's house and knocked repeatedly on the door. No answer. He darted around back to Curtis's window and rapped at it.

"Dang!" Patrick kicked his heels into the grass, shuffled his feet, and returned home.

The next morning, he walked to Curtis's house again. Still, no one answered.

"Dad," Patrick questioned, "Do you know where Curtis's family is?"

"No, son. Maybe on vacation."

"Curtis didn't tell me they had a vacation planned," Patrick said.

"They'll return, don't worry about it," his dad said.

A couple days later, Curtis rode his bicycle over and requested that they head toward a new river trail he had discovered. Patrick climbed on his swirly, girly bike, as Ben called it.

"Where were you? I went over every day!" Patrick inquired.

"Ugh. We took a trip to Texas," Curtis replied.

"What's in Texas?"

"Not much."

"Oh, okay," Patrick said, then dived right in with stories about the national tournament.

Curtis nodded and laughed, taking special interest in the horseshoe crab event. "An animal that looked prehistoric?"

"Yeah," said Patrick. He pulled over by a bend in the river where they could skip rocks.

The boys piled up a load of stones, then set up challenges such as eight skips, or along the edge of the river, or throwing a rock to the other side. With Wildwood memories still fresh in his mind, Patrick longed to go back, but spending time with Curtis felt familiar and content. They discussed pranks and the first day of school. Patrick tried to convince his friend to join Marbles Club.

"I'd join if I could go to nationals," Curtis said.

"Even if you didn't qualify, the games are fun, and we could play them at my house after school."

"Patrick, we have to ride a bus this year," Curtis said changing the subject. "I'll miss our walks to school."

"Yeah, me too."

"What do you think middle school will be like?" Curtis asked.

"I don't know, but I hope we're in the same classes."

Curtis nodded. "My mom wants me home for dinner, so let's ride to the end of this trail before we head back."

"Okay." Patrick pedaled hard feeling his quads burn trying to keep up with Curtis. But that inner strength returned, and he was hopeful for a fantastic sixth grade year.

One evening, a week later, Troy from Tennessee called Patrick to visit. They talked into the night, reminiscing and making plans for the next summer. Thankful for his new friend, he saw a brighter future ahead.

Then tragedy struck. Patrick wandered to Curtis's house to see what he was up to since they hadn't talked in a few days. Peering through the screen door, he saw his friend inside. "Hey, come out." He never felt comfortable inside their house because Curtis's mom scared him.

"Hi, Patrick," Curtis said sitting on the porch.

"What're doing today?"

"Packing," he answered heavily.

"You're going on another vacation?" Patrick asked, surprised. "School starts in three weeks. How long will you be gone?"

"We're not… coming back," Curtis said, looking at Patrick.

"What do you mean?" His heart thumped rapidly.

"We're—we're moving to Texas next week. My dad—he got a job there," Curtis stammered.

Patrick couldn't talk; he couldn't swallow. His eyes filled with tears, and he choked out a sob. Curtis also began to cry. Unable to face each other, they trembled on the cracked concrete porch that they both knew so well. The two steps with weeds shooting up between the seams and the graffiti from years past where they wrote their names in marker. It was all ending.

"You—you can't leave, Curtis!" Patrick finally was able to say as his grief exploded. "You're my best friend—my only friend! What am I going to do without you?"

"At least you'll still know some people when you start school. I'll be completely alone," Curtis said blubbering.

Patrick leaned against his friend's shoulder and sobbed uncontrollably until the tears ran dry.

"I have to pack," Curtis mumbled, pulling himself away from Patrick. He opened the screen door and disappeared inside.

Patrick found his way home despite being in a trance. A new emotion began to stir within him. He noticed his mom at the kitchen table putting on makeup. "Where're you going?" he barked.

Staring at her compact mirror, she answered, "To the gym, Pattycake."

The brief answer grated on his nerves, then he shouted, "Why do you wear makeup to the gym? You're just going to sweat it all off. Oh, I know! You're too worried what all the other women will think of you because of how you look." He shouted louder. "That's all you care about!"

"Pattycake!" his mother called out. Her eyes were round with shock.

"I hate that name!" Patrick raged. "I'm about to turn twelve, and you treat me like a baby. You don't care that it embarrasses me every time you say it! All you care about is what people think of *you*!" He stormed into his room and slammed the door.

Deedee shrieked as if overcome by horror, and she promptly called Chad, ordering him to come home instantly. After that she walked directly into Patrick's room demanding to know the root of his outburst.

"Go away!" he yelled. "Leave me alone!" Patrick shoved a pillow over his face and refused to speak to his mom who was in a state of hysteria at the moment, calling her friends for help and support.

Chad burst into the house believing it had caught on fire or that a plane had crashed into it or something just as awful. Unable to voice her dismay Deedee just pointed at Patrick's door. Chad opened it slowly not knowing what to expect and took stock of the situation. Clothes lay in disarray, broken toys were scattered to and fro, and his son, splayed out on the bed, looked frozen in time.

"Patrick?" Chad asked in a serious tone. "What has happened?"

Patrick slowly tipped his head to one side, taking notice of his dad. He whispered, "Curtis is moving to Texas."

Chad crossed over to the bed, sat down and held his son's hand.

Patrick was so sad he felt like he was going to die, like something was squeezing his heart. His dad tried to comfort him, but no amount of consoling would draw Patrick out of despair this dreadful day. Chad left the room to find Deedee weeping on the sofa. Her makeup, smudged and smeared, ran down her face like paint.

"Honey," Chad said, "Curtis and his family are moving to Texas. Patrick is suffering from grief right now, and although it'll take time, he'll be okay."

"He believes that I'm only concerned about myself and what others think of me," she cried.

"Sometimes the truth must be revealed," said Chad.

Deedee stared at her husband, distraught and angry. "Then, you agree with him?"

"That's the way Patrick sees it, sweetheart. I didn't say that I agree with him."

"There's nothing wrong with wearing makeup when going to the gym," Deedee said. "And I *do* want acceptance from my friends. Have I done something wrong to cause Patrick to harbor such feelings toward me?"

Chad held his tongue, wanting desperately for her to understand that at the moment all she was thinking about *was* herself. "Honey, we need to support our son as he swims through these murky waters. He's hurting." He added, "And I'm sure he'll apologize at some point."

Curtis came over on moving day, and they sobbed again, saying their goodbyes. Then, he left. Gone.

Days passed, and Patrick refused to tell his mom he was sorry. He wouldn't join his parents for dinner. He ate very little, and he chose not to discuss his feelings. Deedee started calling doctors and therapists, worried that her son had fallen into deep, dark depression until finally, Chad walked into Patrick's room.

"Son, I bought something for the two of us to share. I'm asking you to please join me outside."

"I don't want to," Patrick mumbled.

"That's true, and I believe you, but—but I want to," his dad said softly.

Patrick sighed. "What is it?"

"Come see." Chad waited patiently for Patrick to get out of bed.

It took some moments, then Patrick plodded across his room, followed his dad to the garage, and stared blankly at the object. "Share it? Dad, there's only one."

"We both can't ride my new bike. You have one too. We can share the time," his dad said.

"Then, you lied." Patrick frowned. "Dad, I'm not in the mood to ride bikes."

"Well, I want to. Please, son."

He hummed and hawed. "Okay, I guess, for a little while."

"You lead the way. I'll follow," his dad said.

Patrick purposefully took a new route as he couldn't bear to take the trails that he and Curtis shared together. They didn't speak at all. Then, he led his dad home, parked his bike, and shut himself in his room for long periods of time after that.

Sixth grade orientation quickly approached, and Deedee busied herself with preparations. She had been beside herself with Patrick's isolation and sullen demeanor. When she tried to start up a conversation, he'd cover his ears rudely. She finally became fed up with it and put her foot down.

"Patrick—".

"At least you're calling me by name now!" Patrick sneered.

"That's right, and I expect you to show me some respect! I understand that you've had a difficult time without Curtis, but this is a new year. And I want you to start it with a good attitude."

"You don't get it, Mom. School without my best friend is pointless."

"School is *not* pointless," she declared.

Patrick sighed, "That's not what I said."

Deedee, flustered out of her mind, marched away.

That evening, Chad spoke with Patrick privately. "Tomorrow is the orientation, and your mom is under the impression you're not going." He paused. "I want to make something clear to you, son. She did not send Curtis away, so please stop treating her as if it's her fault."

"I'm mad!" Patrick bellowed. "She wants me to get over it, and I can't."

"I don't deny that. I'll be honest with you. This is going to take a while for you to deal with, but you *will* feel happy again someday."

"Ha! What's this got to do with orientation?"

"Actually, not a whole lot, except that having no idea who your teachers are and where to find classrooms may only make life more difficult for you."

"I don't want to go to school this year," Patrick whimpered. "Do I have to?"

"Yes."

Patrick sighed. "Dad, will you go to the orientation with me?"

"Yes."

CHAPTER 18
SIXTH GRADE BLUES

C had asked his employer for the afternoon off so he could go to sixth grade. He told Patrick that his boss laughed and suggested he have a good time and learn a lot. It made Patrick smile slightly. He kept close to his dad as they entered the gymnasium. Deedee felt somewhat uncomfortable in the large crowd of strangers. She secretly wondered if they judged her in one way or another. She had battled with the comments Patrick had made about her and decided she'd try not to be so self-conscious. This tested her intentions to the utmost.

The administrator seemed likeable from the start. He cracked jokes and told funny stories before launching into the serious information, which he kept to a minimum. They divided families into groups by last names for tours. The Melberry's ended up with the Maloney family.

TJ Maloney acted terrified, so when Patrick caught his eye, the old bully turned away quickly. *Maybe he won't have a nickname for me this year*. Patrick wondered doubtfully.

An eighth grader had been chosen to explain the ins and outs of classes, rules, hallway manners, supplies, and lockers. She guided them from room to room and introduced them to the teachers. Then they walked to an outbuilding where band and choir classes were held. Deedee listened intently as the teacher discussed music options over physical education. She noticed Patrick squirming when the girl talked about required PE uniforms.

Eventually, everyone reconvened in the gym for snacks and games. Patrick grabbed a bottle of water and wandered with his dad to a tug of war rope being stretched across the floor. Unevenly matched, several students and their parents selected sides. With one swift jerk, one entire group lost their footing and slid across the mark.

"Let's try," Chad suggested.

Patrick shook his head.

"I think I will, anyway," his dad said, gripping the rope near the knot at the end. Other people took hold in front of him.

Just then, the trio, without their parents, passed by, snickering at Patrick. Then TJ said, "You should grab the knot."

Carlos piped in, "Yeah, take the anchor position."

Finally, Ben shoved his nose into Patrick's face and sneered, "Your team can't lose with the weight of an entire barge at the end."

Patrick felt sick. If he grabbed the knot and they won, he'd be Barge Boy all year. If he didn't, they'd tease him for wimping out. He decided not to satisfy them by doing what they wanted, so he stepped aside and said, "You pick up the knot and do it yourself."

Too late, of course. Chad's team pulled with all their might and defeated their opponents. Deedee clapped enthusiastically. They moved on to more game stations and mostly observed. Patrick witnessed many students reuniting with friends, chatting endlessly about summer vacation and the excitement of middle school. He felt exhausted emotionally and mentally.

"Can we go, now?" he asked.

"Yes, Patty—Patrick, as soon as we receive your paperwork," his mother said.

Long lines formed at a row of tables near the exit door where students obtained locker assignments as well as core and class schedules. He overheard Ben exclaiming that he had been assigned to Blue Heron Core. Deedee handed the folder to Patrick, who didn't bother to inspect the contents until they reached the ice-cream shop. He grumbled.

"You don't want a treat?" Deedee asked disappointedly. "It's a special day."

He was about to dissent, but his dad lifted a wagging finger as if to say, "Do it for your mom."

Patrick recalled this sweet shop. He and Curtis used to see who could suck up the most whipped cream without taking a breath. He had always won. Today, he flung the foamy topping onto the table where it splatted, then spread out like a cloud. Deedee scowled and then wiped it up.

"I'm in Blue Heron Core," Patrick said reading his schedule. He glanced at it looking sullen and sad. "And I have to take PE first semester."

Deedee gasped. "I'll see if I can change it for you."

Patrick was resigned to the fact that sixth grade might just be his doom.

The evening before the first day of school, Chad suggested they pedal their bikes along the river trail. The warm air along with buzzing bugs irritated Patrick but not as much as noticing a tiny pile of skipping rocks still stacked up at their favorite spot by the river. Patrick grabbed his side to pacify the pain of missing his friend. He nearly toppled his bike.

"Do you have a cramp?" his dad called out.

Patrick had to stop, then dump himself from his bike. He doubled over as the sharp jabbing split his ribs. Maybe he felt a cramp, or perhaps the thought of him and Curtis never finishing skipping those rocks was stabbing him to death.

"Take a breather. We're in no hurry, son," said his dad.

He did, and the pain subsided—the physical discomfort, that is. He wondered if a person could literally die from heartache. "Dad, have you ever been as sad as me?"

"Well, my best friend never moved away, but I have felt miserable like you before."

"When?"

"My family adopted a stray dog when I was eight. We named him Boxer. I loved him more than anything, and he loved me. Every day, he waited for me at the bus stop, and every morning he walked me there. Until one day, he didn't." Chad stopped.

"He didn't what?"

"He didn't show up at the bus. When I got home, he was lying in the yard panting. I held his head in my lap till he died. And my heart hurt so horribly that I thought I might die from sadness." Chad sighed. "It's difficult to lose someone. But Patrick, umm, even though Curtis is far away, he's still alive. You're still his friend, and he's yours. You'll see him again."

"I guess," Patrick said shrugging his shoulders.

The next morning, Patrick vomited. He hadn't slept all night due to tormenting dreams about walking into sixth grade naked, having his head swirled in a toilet, being forced to share a locker with Carlos, and being stabbed with a real dagger. Deedee fussed over him but was unable to send him to school due to illness protocol. She worried to the point of giving herself a headache, so she had to lay down. The first day of school passed uneventfully, but he'd have to go eventually.

The next morning, Patrick missed his bus, so his mom drove and had to check him in as tardy at the office. The first period of the day was, of course, PE, so his teacher handed him a much-too-small uniform. He had to wear his school clothes and so he stood out like a sore thumb. The students pointed at him and snickered, sharing insults under their breaths. The computer lab, a room too tiny for such a large class, had been crammed full of students bumping elbows with their neighbor. Patrick was situated between two girls who thought it amusing to take turns poking the rolls of his belly with their fingers while he attempted to type.

The cafeteria posed a problem in that Patrick's account hadn't updated so he had to charge his first sixth grade meal after enduring a scolding by the lunch lady. The day wore on like this until his last period, literacy, where he was seated next to Ben.

"Hi," Ben said, acknowledging Patrick.

"What?" Patrick asked puzzled.

"I don't know anyone in this class except you," Ben said.

"So what?"

"TJ and Carlos are in the other core," explained Ben.

"Oh."

"How's Curtis?" Ben asked, seeming to show interest.

Patrick felt at a loss. Ben shouldn't even be talking to him. They were enemies. And he hadn't considered the fact that Curtis may be sitting all alone in a room somewhere in Texas right now. He stared at Ben dubiously then focused on the whiteboard not giving him a second thought.

After school, hundreds of students funneled into buses. Patrick hadn't taken the time to learn his bus number, so he paced back and forth, peering up into windows in search of anyone he might recognize that lived in his neighborhood. Kids rapped on the windows and pressed their noses against it so all he could see was the black holes of their nostrils. Then, a student slid his window down and poked his head out.

"Hey, Melberry!" Ben shouted. "There's an empty seat just for you at the front of the bus. You'd never be able to squeeze your way down the aisle."

"Shut up!" Patrick yelled.

"Too bad for you that Curtis isn't here to defend you. Yeah, I saw the moving truck."

Patrick glared at Ben. His eyes began to swell with tears.

Ben laughed. "Oh, poor baby, Patrick. You lost your pacifier, and he's never coming back."

Patrick turned and walked away, stumbling over a sprinkler head that had not been pushed back into the grass. He fell flat on his stomach. Laughter broke out from all directions. He felt sure he heard Ben shout something about a walrus. Patrick pounded his fist into the moist sod, then lifted himself up to his hands and knees. His shirt and pants were wet from the grass, making it look as if he'd slobbered profusely down his chest and perhaps even peed his pants.

A bit later, as Patrick debated whether he should get up and catch the bus or remain in the grass, a gentle hand rested on his shoulder.

"Patrick," she said calmly.

He recognized her voice but couldn't place it. "What?" he asked, feeling humiliated.

"Patrick, I'm sorry you're having a bad day."

Lifting his head, he realized that Lissy, the girl who accompanied the Colorado team to the national tournament, was looking at him with soft eyes and a slight frown. She knelt down beside him.

"I saw how those kids on the bus treated you," Lissy said. "That's plain cruel."

"Yeah," Patrick replied.

"Do you need a ride home?"

"What?"

"Or do you still want to catch your bus? They're about to leave," said Lissy.

"I'll walk," he answered.

"Where do you live?" Lissy asked.

Patrick sat back on his heels and stared at her. She seemed worried—not the same girl he remembered from Wildwood.

There, she smiled a whole lot. Shy, yes, but he recalled her happiness and wished they were back at the boardwalk where people liked him.

"My parents give me a ride home every day, and I'm sure they could take you home too," Lissy said.

"I guess," Patrick said as the buses pulled away. Ben continued his jeering until he was out of sight.

"Where's your friend? The one with the crazy orange hair. Did he already get on the bus?" she asked.

"He moved," he said bluntly.

"That's sad. I'm sorry."

"I don't want to talk about it," Patrick said, standing up.

Lissy walked toward a bench and sat down to wait for her ride. Patrick considered joining her, but he didn't want to bum a ride off of someone when he was angry. He just stood there motionless. A silver car drove in to the pick-up zone. Lissy waved at him to come over, but he was still like cement.

"Patrick!" she called.

"I—I need time to think things through," he said. "Thanks for the offer, but I'll just walk."

"Are you sure?"

"Yeah, it's not far," Patrick said waving them off. But it was far. Miles even. He'd never walked that distance, nor had he ever ridden his bike such a long way. His ill temper combined with loneliness resulted in a pitiful predicament. "Dummy, Patrick," he said to himself. "Now you have to pay the price."

As he shuffled his feet, he struck a pebble. His first reaction was to kick it over to Curtis as they so often did in the past, but instead, he bent over, picked it up, and threw it with all his might. Then he balled up his fist and shook it at the sky, demanding a reason as to why his life was so miserable. Eventually, he took another step, and then another—blotting out his thoughts and feelings and concentrating only on stepping.

Over an hour later, he arrived at his front porch with blistered feet and a pounding heart. His lungs choked for air. A minute later, Deedee abruptly opened the front door, obviously upset and worried.

"Mom," he quickly inserted before she could speak, "I missed the bus and decided to walk home."

"Patrick, I drove around for thirty minutes looking for you! I almost called the police!"

"Well, I didn't take the main road," said Patrick. "I walked the path by the river."

"How could you miss the bus? Didn't they let you out in time? Do you know your bus number? What about other kids in our neighborhood? Couldn't you have followed them to the correct bus?" Deedee, flustered as she was, attempted to solve the problem. "The teachers need to let students out earlier, or the bus drivers need to have an attendance list to check off." Her exasperation carried on.

Patrick tolerated her tirade until she calmed down enough to see to it that he was okay. Then her demeanor changed to worrisome as she fretted over his bleeding feet. He let her because they seriously stung, and it was all he could do not to cry out when she trimmed the loose skin around the broken blisters. Finally, he crashed onto his bed with bandages on his feet.

That evening, Patrick could hear his parents whispering in the living room. He desperately desired to eavesdrop, but he didn't dare place his sore feet on the floor. Then, the full moon sent forth its shining glow through his bedroom window casting black shadows that reminded him of the grim reaper. He finally drifted off into a fretful slumber.

"Ow!" Patrick shrieked when he tried to slip out of bed and walk to the bathroom the next morning. "Mom!" he cried.

Deedee rushed to his aid but didn't have the strength to carry him. He knew that of course, but he appreciated the gesture.

"It's okay, Mom, I'll crawl."

Deedee began to sob. "Oh Pattycake, you won't make it to

school today, and you've already missed the first day. I don't want you to fall behind."

Grumbling, Patrick exclaimed, "I think my feet are more important than school, don't you?"

Deedee wept even more! In fact, it seemed to Patrick that she spent a good deal of time crying these days. She strode out of his room and down the hallway, then he found a way to maneuver himself around the bathroom and back to his bed where the day passed achingly slow. His blisters burned and his heart felt heavy. He longed to see Curtis, his better half, his true friend who was so far gone from his life.

Patrick missed the next day of school as well. Deedee cried. And Chad came home from work with a small box, which he presented to his son.

"Your mom and I decided to give you an early birthday present." He grinned expectantly.

"Wow! Is this?" Patrick tore open the box and out spilled a phone. "Mine?"

"Yes, it's yours, with limits, of course," Chad explained.

"Awesome! Thanks!"

His dad left him alone to discover the ins and outs of this new electronic device. It kept him occupied for a good amount of time until he realized that it was after midnight. He figured he'd waddle around school the next day since his feet had improved, although he dreaded attending. At least his mom planned on driving him.

"Patrick Melberry," his PE teacher said. "This uniform should suffice. I expect students to dress out before class starts, and you're already running behind."

Thankful that the teacher and the other boys had departed the locker room, Patrick quickly threw the shirt over his head and jumped into the shorts. "Ugh. No, more like ugh-ly. Who wears such ridiculous clothes?" Patrick wasn't prepared to rush around the field kicking a soccer ball, so he offered to serve as goalie, except that he was horrible at it. He blocked zero goals, and a ball smacked him in the face at least once. His teammates shook their heads and belittled him.

After Patrick stuffed his stinky PE uniform into his gym locker and dressed back into his school clothes, he wandered the halls searching for his next class. Rather than being mocked for showing up late, he spent the next period in the restroom playing with soap bubbles. He discovered that missing two days of school meant a whole week of catch-up homework, which he didn't intend to do as he could barely make sense out of today's assignments.

Finally, lunch arrived. Hungry and irritated, he took his tray to a corner of the cafeteria and sat down. A few moments later, Gail and a new friend of hers approached his table, said hello, and took a seat near him. He squirmed uncomfortably.

"Patrick, how is the year for you so far?" Gail asked sweetly.

He didn't mean for it to slip out, but it did. "Curtis moved away!"

"I know, I heard. That must be sad for you," she said. "Is he doing alright?"

"Well, I haven't heard from him yet," Patrick explained.

"Have you tried calling him?"

"No, he doesn't have a phone, and I don't want to call his parents," Patrick answered, grimacing at the thought of speaking to Curtis's mom.

"That's too bad," Gail said sincerely. She went on to tell him about her summer and that she painted a few more rabbits from *Watership Down*. "TJ and Carlos are in my core, and they've found new kids to pick on. Is Ben still bullying you?"

"Yes." He felt strange talking to her about being teased especially with her new friend listening in, so he changed the subject and told her about the National Marbles Tournament. She listened with intrigue and giggled at his stories. Lunch ended much too soon. He wished she was in at least one of his classes.

During literacy class, Patrick asked to be moved to a different spot in the room in order to prevent Ben from bothering him constantly. Luckily, his teacher obliged. He tried to pay attention to her lecture, but his mind wandered to the bus ride home. When the bell rang, he made a point to avoid the crowd of students. With head down, he strolled to his bus and sat in the first empty seat near the driver and slumped so low that it appeared the seat was vacant.

CHAPTER 19
MIXED EMOTIONS

One evening while Chad and Patrick rode their bikes along the river, Patrick's phone buzzed. No one had ever called him.

"Hello," Patrick said.

The voice on the other end was Mrs. Lee. "Patrick, I want to personally invite you to Marbles for Fun Club, which starts next week."

"Oh, okay," he answered. He abruptly said goodbye and hung up feeling awkward talking on his new phone.

Chad said, "Hey, that sounds like she really wants you to join again."

Patrick thought about it yet said nothing.

When they returned home, Deedee was crying and wailing about a piece of paper she held in her shaking hand.

"What's wrong, sweetheart?" Chad asked, pulling her close and read the words. "Patrick, your school administrator wants a meeting with us. It says here that your grades are failing and that you're missing classes during the day."

"I don't know why. I try to keep up with my homework," he said sheepishly.

"Well, let's not get riled up about it until we see what he has to say tomorrow afternoon," Chad said.

Deedee ran to the bathroom, feeling sick. Patrick felt bad that he caused his mom so much grief, but she just couldn't understand how hard life was for him these days. Chad gently pulled him to another room.

"Your mom is having a difficult time," Chad began.

Patrick interrupted, "I'm trying, Dad, but things are too tough for me. I hate school, Curtis is gone, and I have no friends. Now, I'm getting Fs, and the principal is mad at me!"

"Yes, that all adds flames to the fire," he said. "She has been very sick and emotional."

"Well, it's not my fault she's so upset all the time," he declared.

"Son, if you'll stop and listen for a minute. I have something important to tell you." He paused. "Your mom is pregnant!"

"What?" Patrick burst out laughing. "No, she's not! You're kidding me, right?"

"Not at all, son. She's going to have a baby next May!"

A dump truck of confusion unloaded its contents on Patrick's head and heart. He couldn't wrap his brain around the news, and he didn't know how to feel—jealousy crept in along with curiosity. The two mixed together about as well as gum and nuts. He was mad at the world for shoving such a difficult life down his throat, but he also felt love—certainly not for himself, but for a person, an unknown part of his family that would change everything.

Patrick was dumbfounded. "Dad?"

"Yes?" Chad responded.

"I don't know what to do," he said bemused.

"I understand."

"I wish I could talk to Curtis," Patrick whined. "How can I talk to him, Dad?"

"I wouldn't suggest you call his mom or dad. Be patient. Curtis is adjusting to many changes right now. He knows our number and will call you soon enough." Chad looked directly into Patrick's eyes. "And you have many burdens you're carrying as well. I know that, and I'm here for you, son."

At dinner, Patrick couldn't stop staring at his mom. She looked frazzled and pale. He worried about her and the baby. And he worried about the meeting with the principal. *Would she attend? What if she throws up? What if I throw up?*

"Pattycake. I mean Patrick," Deedee said solemnly, "Pregnancy isn't a disease. I'm going to be okay, so stop looking at me like that."

"Uh, oh, yeah, okay," he stammered.

His head hurt and his mind was a tornado. "I'm going to bed early," Patrick announced.

The covers pulled up to his chin, eyes wide open, he stared blankly at the ceiling trying to organize his thoughts. He felt dizzy. "Hey, Curtis," he spoke out loud pretending his friend could hear, "My life stinks!" He considered Curtis's answer. "I know your life must be awful too. Why haven't you called me?" He paused. "You don't have a phone. That's why. What good does it do to have a phone when I have no friends?" He waited. "Am I still your best friend?"

Patrick gave up on his imaginary conversation with Curtis. He seriously contemplated dialing Curtis's mom's number, but pushed his phone under his pillow. "That's only as a last resort." He tiptoed to the end of the hallway and listened to his parents discussing his grades.

"Deedee, I understand. You haven't felt well enough to check on Patrick's daily schoolwork, so please don't be so hard on yourself," Chad said.

"We can't let this go on!" she said. "We'll hire a tutor if necessary."

"Ugh," Patrick grunted. "Can life suck any more than it already does?" He padded quietly back to his bedroom and dug through his desk drawer. "Where is it?" Shoving his pudgy hand deep into the mess, he found what he searched for. Rolling the bumble bee shooter between thumb and index finger, Patrick relaxed somewhat as shadowy glimpses of Wildwood bounced off his brain. He tried to imagine himself on the rings, in the sand, on the rollercoasters, but the memories had dulled over time as if years had come between him and those pleasant feelings. Sometime in the middle of the night, the bumble bee fell from his fingers and dropped to the floor where it rolled under his bed while Patrick slept.

Another dreadful day of sixth grade grated on Patrick's already singed nerves, and the meeting hung over his head like a deadly sword. He hoped that Gail would've joined him for lunch again, but she only waved from a distance. Alone, always alone, he nibbled at his food. By himself, when everyone else walked in groups, he shuffled his feet from room to room. In the back of literacy class, he heard Ben's spiteful whispers. Then, his parents arrived, and he soberly made his way to the principal's office.

"Welcome, Mr. and Mrs. Melberry," the administrator said. "Come sit with us, Patrick." He set several sheets of paper on his desk for all to see—his grades, a contract of some sort, and colorful cardstock with lists of healthy learning behaviors.

Patrick slumped sullenly waiting for the axe to drop. Chad leaned forward to read the papers while Deedee attempted to keep her composure, either from sickness or from shame and embarrassment.

The principal pointed out the problems, suggested helpful tips, and basically left the Melberry family with no choice but to dive into the deep end of improving or else. Or else never come up for air and drown. At least that's what Patrick took away from the meeting.

"We can do this, Patrick," Chad said. "Together, as a family we'll work this out, son."

"Pull over, Chad," Deedee demanded as she leaned out her window ready to vomit.

Patrick groaned.

Deedee had hired a tutor two days a week. Chad spent his evenings relearning sixth grade math and science and spent more time than Patrick reading history books and helping him write research papers. The days passed foggily, and the nights grew drearier until one Monday after school Lissy and her mom caught up with Patrick before he climbed on his bus.

"Your mom texted you. Did you get it?" Lissy asked.

"No," Patrick said. He rarely checked his phone.

"She wanted us to take you to Marbles Club today. Mrs. Lee has been wanting you to come back."

"Oh, well, I didn't register for it, and I don't have my marbles sock," Patrick said.

"Mrs. Lee knows, but she'll let you join any time, and you can borrow marbles from me," Lissy replied.

He didn't feel up to it, knowing that he'd have to stay up late doing catch-up work. "Maybe another time."

Lissy's mom intervened. "Patrick, I think Mrs. Lee has something special for you, maybe a surprise. She didn't want us to tell you. Will you please come with us at least for today?"

"Yeah, I guess." He sat in the back seat feeling awkward.

Stepping into the gym brought a flood of emotions. He choked up and swallowed hard. He'd missed this. Leigh jumped up and high-fived him within seconds, and the two of them chattered nonstop until Mrs. Lee started speaking.

"We'll head outside today to dig holes in the dirt," she said. "We're playing Poison, or some people like to call the game Black Snake. All you need is your shooter."

Leigh wasted no time passing a brown, speckled marble to Patrick. "Use this. It was my first shooter, and it's perfect for Poison. You'll see why."

Using sticks and their fingernails, the kids hollowed out two-inch wide depressions in the ground zigzagging the holes in a long *S* formation like a snake. The head of the snake was the poison hole. Anyone who navigated their shooter into each dug-out consecutively and finally reached the end became poison and could aim at and hit any other player's marble and make them start over again.

"Now, I see," Patrick whispered to Leigh, "Your brown shooter is the same color as the dirt, so if someone is poison, my marble will be camouflaged, and I won't get knocked out."

"Yep," Leigh agreed.

Patrick enjoyed himself immensely and pouted when club ended. "I'll try to come back next Monday," he told Leigh and Lissy. Then he ventured to Mrs. Lee who waved him over.

"I've wondered about you," Mrs. Lee said. "I've heard about the difficult year you've had. Your mom contacted me, saying she thought you needed a day off of schoolwork, so she signed you up for Marbles Club."

"She did? That *is* a huge surprise!"

"How're you doing, Patrick?"

"I'm good—no. I'm—I'm not," he said looking at her. "My best friend moved, my mom is pregnant and sick all of the time, and sixth grade is the worst!"

"I'm sorry about that," she said. Smiling, she added, "Today, you seemed happily entertained."

"Yes, I was!"

"You have friends here, you know?"

Patrick nodded. "Yes," he said.

"Then, I'll see you next week," she said patting his shoulder.

When Lissy's mom dropped him off at his house, Deedee had just entered the bathroom. Patrick missed her after school hugs and baked cookies. He wouldn't admit it, but he longed to hear her say Pattycake every now and then, simply to feel her warmth toward him. Now, she didn't have the energy to go to the gym, hang out with her friends, or even wear makeup. *What in the world was this baby doing to her*, he wondered?

"Hi, Dad," Patrick said when Chad stepped in the door.

"Hello, son. Where's your mom?"

Patrick pointed to the bathroom.

Chad's shoulders slumped. It bothered him, too.

"I went to Marbles Club today," he said.

"Wonderful! We thought we'd add a bright spot in your week. Was it?"

"Yeah. But we still have homework to do, right?"

Chad answered, "No, Mondays are free days from now on."

A small weight fell from Patrick's shoulders. Although, he still felt like a train engine pulling heavy cars behind him. Midterms came out earlier that month. A few of his grades had improved, but he still failed literacy. His dad appeared exhausted. After a long day of work, he took care of Patrick's mom and then burned the midnight oil helping with homework. Patrick was keenly aware that his own efforts weren't his best, and deep inside, he held on to a bitter attitude toward life and himself. Amidst the monotonous pattern, at least he found some relief on Mondays.

Weeks passed, and one Saturday morning, a moving truck pulled into the driveway of Curtis's old home. Patrick's skin burned as the blood boiled in his veins. "How dare you ruin my memories!" he shouted at the truck. "Get out of here!" Tears spilled unwillingly as he yelled at the intruders. Another vehicle parked behind the mover's vehicle. Patrick assumed the newcomers were excited about their new home, and without real-izing it, he clenched his fists ready to fight anyone who stepped foot into Curtis's old house. Suddenly, a tall boy with wild orange hair sprinted in his direction with a most determined coun-tenance.

"Patrick!" Curtis screeched with delight. He slammed into him tackling him to the ground playfully.

"What are you doing?" Patrick shouted. "Are you moving back?" He sat up staring at his best friend as if he was dreaming.

"Oh, I wish! Our house sold, and we had to return to finalize something—I don't know what. And my dad wanted to meet with the buyers for some reason. Does it matter? I'm here for a couple of days!"

"Wow!" Patrick shoved Curtis into the grass, and they wrestled like second graders except that his friend's arms and legs had grown so awkwardly long that he had trouble gaining an advantage.

"Have you lost weight?" Curtis asked. "You're stronger than I remember."

"Well, you're a monkey, now!" Patrick said laughing.

"You wouldn't believe what I've gone through," Curtis began. "The very first day of school, I got busted for sticking a wad of gum in a girl's ponytail. The principal suspended me for two days, and I had to see the counselor every week!"

"Really?" Patrick's jaw dropped.

"That's not the worst. My mom literally put bars on my bedroom window and set up a security system around our whole house," Curtis said growling. "I painted the bars bright orange one night."

"What? Why?"

"I'll tell you! I met a kid smarter than anyone we'd ever met in our whole lives. I promised I'd give him two dollars a day if he did my homework for me. Oh, I forgot, I started mowing lawns. Anyway, our house is identical to all the others in our neighborhood—a really weird thing, don't you think?"

"For sure," Patrick agreed.

"He knew to look for the orange bars. He slipped my finished assignments to me, and I slipped my new homework to him with the money," Curtis said as he smiled mischievously. "And it worked for a few weeks until we had to take midterms. Did you take them too?"

"Uh," Patrick replied, quite fascinated with Curtis's story.

"Can you guess? Well, I flunked them horribly, so my teachers somehow caught wind of me cheating. Don't worry, the kid never got caught, but that ended our homework transfers."

Patrick asked, "Then what happened?"

"My mom went crazy. I'm not kidding you. She had to be treated at a mental hospital and start taking medications for something called skit-zo-fren-ya, or something like that. My dad took the bars off my windows and shut down the spy system in our house. He kind of spent a lot of time keeping his eye on Mom from then on."

"Really? Is she okay?"

"Yeah, she is now. But the docs think she needs a respite from me, so any chance I get, I leave the house and go do something. Mostly, I mow lawns and ride my bike. And I got to come here and see you!"

"Awesome!" Patrick's heart swelled with joy. Then he took on a more serious tone. "Do you have any new friends?"

"Na. Well, I guess there's a couple guys that I see at the bike park. They don't go to my school, though." Curtis asked, "What about you? How's everything here?"

Patrick went into detail about his miserable life, and how awful it'd been without Curtis there. "And my mom is pregnant," he added.

"No way!" Curtis exclaimed. "When?"

"In May," Patrick replied.

"Boy or girl?"

"I don't know," Patrick answered, wondering why he never even thought about that part. Changing the subject, he said, "Hey! Let's ride bikes to our old favorite places. You can borrow my dad's new bicycle."

"You bet!" Curtis quickly got permission from his dad, and the two of them ventured off as if nothing had changed between them in the past few months.

CHAPTER 20
A WORD FROM GOD

When Curtis left the second time, Patrick fell back into grief, anger, and depression. No matter how much his dad encouraged him to keep up with schoolwork, he just couldn't muster up the motivation. They allowed him to continue playing marbles, however, which brought some satisfaction each week. In addition, Leigh commenced plans for competitive practice in his garage.

"Patrick, I'm going to try to win nationals this year. Mrs. Lee wrote out percentages I'd need to meet to have a chance at the championship. Look at this," Leigh said, showing Patrick the list.

"That's totally impossible!" Patrick exclaimed. "Ninety percent accuracy at everything you shoot at?"

"Yeah, I know. I'm asking you to hold me accountable for practices and tell me jokes to keep me laughing every now and then." Leigh looked at Patrick sincerely. "Will you?"

"Yeah, sure," he answered.

"Great! Let's start next Wednesday. What do you say?"

Patrick nodded, hoping that his parents would allow another

free day from schoolwork. He intended to mention it to them that evening figuring they'd put the hammer down on that one.

"Dad, Leigh asked me to be his marbles practice partner again," Patrick said later that day. "Every Wednesday. May I do it," he asked.

Patrick's dad knew the strain sixth grade was having on his son, and the stress of having a sibling, so he responded, "Yes, I think that would be healthy for you."

"Whew! Thanks, Dad!" Patrick said. He found his brown agate and began to roll it between his fingers.

Wednesday arrived, and Patrick decided he rather liked crawling around on his hands and knees in the crowded garage. A new layer of sandy paint had been applied to the ring, so the aggies stuck nicely when shot with backspin.

"Have you thought about going back to Wildwood next summer," Leigh asked.

"I'd like to, but I haven't practiced at all, and my mom's baby is due the month before, so I doubt I could participate," Patrick replied.

"That's exciting and sad at the same time. Are you going to practice with me at all?"

"I guess so. A little. Mostly, I'll catch your runaway mibs," Patrick said. Hence, Wednesdays resulted in amazing progress for Leigh, while Patrick tried his best to make him laugh.

On the last Marbles Club Monday of the semester, Mrs. Lee asked Patrick to stay for a bit as she wanted to speak to his mom, who felt well enough that day to pick him up. He'd ridden home with Lissy and her mom most of autumn, and although he appreciated the rides, she and her mom hardly carried a conversation for more than two sentences. He always felt a bit uncomfortable.

"Hello, Mrs. Melberry," Mrs. Lee said. "I'm thrilled to see that you're up to driving again. I've heard this pregnancy has kept you confined to your house."

"Yes, I've suffered quite a bit, but I'm hoping the nausea will pass, soon," she said. Deedee turned to Patrick and embraced him gently so as not to embarrass him in front of the other kids still waiting for their parents.

Patrick didn't blush, which surprised him, and he said, "Hi, Mom."

"I'd like to ask your permission to take Patrick to an elderly gentleman's house Saturday morning. He has something he wants to show your son," said Mrs. Lee.

"I'm okay with that, but please talk to my husband about the details. I don't know how I'll feel this weekend."

Patrick burned with anticipation the whole week. He awoke Saturday morning red hot with excitement. *I wonder who he is and what he has*, he thought as he slipped a cleaner shirt than normal over his head and brushed cat hair off his pants.

Mrs. Lee knocked on the door, then he and his dad climbed into her white truck and sped away to the other side of the city—a thirty-minute drive on side streets. As they drove she explained the situation. "I received a phone call from a woman who read about our marbles club in the newspaper last summer. She invited me to their home and told me a sentimental story about her husband."

"She introduced me to her husband who told me that his life was fading away." She paused. "Sad."

"We're going to a dying man's house?" Patrick asked, feeling creeped out.

"That's right, Patrick. And he has something he wants to show you before he passes. I hope he'll convey the same story he shared with me, but he's weak and tired, so we'll see," she said as they pulled into the driveway.

"Oh, gosh!" Patrick exclaimed. "I'm nervous, now." His palms began to sweat, and his knees shook a little as they clambered out of the truck and up the steep porch steps. A shabby screen door hung loosely on the hinges, while cracked Christmas ornaments dangled from the handle. A faded welcome sign was attached to the wooden door behind the screen.

Mrs. Lee rang a doorbell. The sound of musical chimes echoed inside the house. "It'll take a moment," she said.

Patrick searched the premises with wide eyes. The place carried memories—old children's tractors with rusty sidewalls lay partly hidden under a thin blanket of snow. A bicycle with no tires hung from a set of hooks in the carport, and stacks and stacks of old magazines lined a shelf next to the bike. In the yard was a bird bath tipped to one side and partially full of dirty frozen water. A weathered fence was tangled between overgrown tree trunks.

A bent figure appeared in the doorway. As the woman opened the door, a wave of warm air escaped. She greeted Mrs. Lee and motioned them inside. Her thin, wrinkled smile was welcoming, yet her tiny frame wobbled as she made her way to the kitchen table where yellowing doilies showed place settings for two. Her soft, cracking voice caught Patrick off guard.

"You must be the young mibster Mrs. Lee told me about?"

He glanced at Mrs. Lee who confirmed her statement. "Yes, I'm Patrick Melberry," he said, returning a smile.

"My husband looks forward to meeting you," the frail woman said. "I'll get him. He's been resting." With that, she left the kitchen and faded away into a shadowy room across the way.

"What did you tell her about me?" Patrick asked anxiously.

"I told her and her husband that you're special, and that you'd understand," Mrs. Lee answered.

"Understand?" Patrick was perplexed.

Moments later, a tall, aged man limped awkwardly into the room. He wore a frayed flannel shirt with missing buttons, and beneath that, an old white t-shirt stuck out at the collarbone. His head, nearly bald, showed years of sun exposure while his thin-skinned hands exposed red blood spots. Tucked tightly to his chest, he carried a rectangular cigar box which he set very carefully on top of a doily.

"Sit down, please," he told Patrick. The old gentleman placed his palms on the edge of the table and lowered himself onto a cushion resting on a kitchen chair. He lifted his foggy grayish green eyes and stared at Patrick through wire-rimmed spectacles. "Do you know how old I am, son?"

"No, sir," Patrick said, finding politeness from somewhere inside himself.

"I've lived ninety-seven blessed years!" he said. His cracked lips turned up to create a partial smile. "Two months ago, I had a stroke, and today, I look forward to my eternal home in Heaven."

Patrick stared at the dying man, at a loss for a response.

"You see this place? All this stuff?" he waved his arm in an arc. "This house and everything in it, the yard out there and that old Chevy sitting in the driveway? Well, I can't take any of it with me." The man stopped, coughed, and caught his breath. "My wife and I, we have two sons and countless grandchildren and great grand-children. Are you following me?" he asked Patrick.

"Yes, yes I am," said Patrick wondering what the man was getting at and feeling sad for this person's family.

"Do you know what a will is for?" Without waiting for Patrick to answer, he went on. "It designates which family members inherit, or get to have, all of this stuff I've accumulated over my lifetime."

The man's wife nodded with exasperation as if she felt over-whelmed by the distribution of so many material items sitting around and tucked away in dark closets. "We have truly been blessed and we're grateful."

Suddenly, his piercing eyes dug into Patrick's soul. "Not every-thing was written in my will. What's in this box was left out, because I know my sons and their children. They don't want it. It doesn't mean anything to them except old stories." He rapped the cardboard with his knuckles. "No, this treasure box holds my fondest memories. My childhood identity and an old man's cares fill the space inside."

He hesitantly pushed the box toward Patrick. "Open it, and see what precious pearls peer back at you."

Patrick gently lifted the lid. A musty smell escaped, an ancient odor, like the inside of Mr. Jerry's old garage. Scattered amongst crumpled up tissue and flattened cotton balls, his precious marbles lay there motionless. Patrick's eyes lit up as he gazed at the amazing marbles, orbs that lived—lived to be touched like Mr. Seitler's desk marbles, and to be rolled between the fingers, and flicked with power and spin into dug out holes in the dirt.

The gentleman shrieked with exuberance. "You *do* understand!" He slammed his hand on the table with great satisfaction. "I see it in your eyes, young man! Go ahead. Take them out."

Patrick fondled each one, finally pinching a green agate between his thumb and index finger. He squeezed it tightly and flicked it with backspin on the table where it spun brightly like the earth in a dark universe. He grinned with admiration and appreciation, lifting his eyes to the old man.

"That one was my favorite aggie," he said smiling crookedly. "You, child, have allowed me to die in peace. When that is, I don't know. But the part of me that runs in my blood will run in yours from now on. I find you worthy of these marbles, and I want you to take them home with you."

Patrick stared at the deeply cracked lines in his face, eyes that shone a little brighter, and white whiskery stubble about his chin. "Why me?"

"I was a mibster in my youth. Not a day went by that I didn't carry my pouch of marbles at my side. I beat the other boys so often that they called me Mr. Marbles, and I won hundreds and hundreds of their best mibs. I counted and polished them, washed them when they were covered in dirt, and set others aside for only special occasions and games. I continued to play when others outgrew the game, and as I moved around as a young man, I left plenty of items behind but not these. I taught my lovely wife to shoot marbles and some of our most memorable times were playing marbles together. When our sons were old enough to hold an aggie, I couldn't wait to teach them as well and share my pastime with them. They weren't interested." He dropped his eyes for a moment. "I promised myself that when I witnessed the light sparkling from a young boy's eyes at the sight of my treasured marbles, then I'd know I could let them go. You're that boy!"

Chad gasped.

Patrick's heart beat rapidly, his throat grew tight, and his eyes filled with tears. He stood up, still clenching the green agate in his hand, and wrapped his arms around the man's neck and shoulders. He felt the years melt between them as if the generation gap dissolved due to a common love.

"Thank you, sir! Thank you very much!" Patrick said, stepping away from the embrace. "I will take care of them. I promise."

"Play with them, Patrick," the gentleman replied. "Keep the legacy alive. It's a dying sport you know—marbles—but even if there's just a handful of kids like you, it'll never die out." He seemed to lose energy after that as if this short conversation had worn him out. Then, he excused himself and shuffled past the living room and into the shadows of the house.

Mrs. Lee spoke a few quiet words to the elderly woman who smiled gratefully, and then they stepped out into the wintry cold. Patrick stole a glance at the unkempt house and yard as they drove away. He held the musty-smelling cigar box in his lap and considered not only the worth of the marbles but his own worth as well.

That next Wednesday, Patrick decided to practice with Leigh. He pulled out the well-used green aggie and rolled it between his fingers. "Look, Leigh," he said showing him his new shooter. "I like this one better than my old brown one." He went on to tell the story of how he came to own it. "He told me I was worthy of them—even more than his own sons."

Leigh stopped flicking his shooter and peered at Patrick.

"What?" Patrick asked staring back.

"You're not worthy because someone decided to give you his old, loved marbles, Patrick."

"What do you mean I'm not?"

"That's not where your value comes from. Yeah, you'll keep playing marbles and tell his story over and over, but if you lost all those marbles and forgot his story, you'd still be somebody important," Leigh explained.

"To whom? You?" Patrick asked.

"Yeah, of course, me," Leigh said smiling. "Okay, don't think I'm preaching, but you know how I told you I pray to Jesus to help me with my games? Not so I can win, but so I know He's with me?"

"Yeah, I remember," Patrick said, but he was puzzled.

"He's not just some God out there that looks down at people as they do all their daily things. He wants to be a part of it all. You told me that the old man said he was ready to go to Heaven, right?"

"That's what he said," Patrick answered.

"Not everyone goes to Heaven when they die." Leigh paused. "People who believe that God sent his Son, Jesus, to show people the way to Heaven are the ones that go there."

"What's the way, then?" asked Patrick.

"Do you ever do anything wrong?" Leigh asked.

"Yes, sometimes."

"Do you believe Jesus died to forgive you for those things?"

"No," Patrick replied.

"Then, according to the Bible, you won't go to Heaven," said Leigh.

"Um," Patrick mumbled. "I don't get it."

"I believe that when Jesus came to earth, he came for one purpose and that was to die as a sacrifice for our sins since nobody can be good enough to earn their way to Heaven. Someone had to take the punishment that we deserve."

"My parents ground me," Patrick said, trying to make sense of what Leigh described.

"Mine too," Leigh responded with a frown. "That's not the punishment I'm talking about. Jesus is the only way to Heaven, and all the stuff you do wrong has to be forgiven by Jesus first. He loves you and values you enough that he took your punishment for you. That's where your worth comes from. If you believe it, He forgives you."

"I've never heard about Jesus before except for at Christmas," Patrick said. "I didn't know any of that."

"Well," explained Leigh, "If you start reading the Bible, you'll learn more. You can ask me, but I still have tons to learn myself."

"I don't have a Bible."

"You can have one of ours. We have extras," said Leigh.

With that, they flicked for backspin one hundred times before attempting the percentage list that Mrs. Lee had given Leigh. Marbles practice was difficult that day. Patrick had a lot on his mind. For one, he had decided to practice enough to qualify for the National Marbles Tournament, and he looked forward to it.

CHAPTER 21
MAKING CHOICES

A gift arrived in the mail two days before Christmas. Patrick didn't wait to open it since it was from Curtis. He ripped open the box and out spilled two items and a note, which read:

Hi Patrick! Merry Christmas. My mom got put in a mental hospital, so it's just me and Dad, now. It's been weird. My grades are better since I had to get a tutor, but he's nice. I think I'm getting a phone for Christmas, so we can talk all the time, and that will be awesome! There's a girl I like in seventh grade. Her name is Lila, and we meet up at the bus stop and sometimes sit together. Do you have a girlfriend? I miss you and hanging out with you and especially all the pranks we played. Here's a pack of bubble gum, and a cool marble that my dad bought online. Have a good Christmas, Curtis.

Patrick studied the large glass sphere inside the zipped, plastic bag. A piece of paper labeled it as a latticino core swirl. Inside the clear glass, a swirl of twisted yellow threads wound their way from one edge of the marble to the other. Near the outside of the glass, white and green ribbons of color wound around the sphere. Under the label, in tiny letters, it said it was handmade in Germany.

"Wow, this is pretty!" Patrick exclaimed. Then without thinking, he stuffed a few pieces of gum in his cheek.

Deedee's nausea still bothered her but seemed to improve as the day went on. She sat beside Patrick after he opened his gift. "What did Curtis send?" she asked.

He held it up to her. "It's worth a lot of money, probably," Patrick said, slobbering.

"That's really beautiful!"

"Yeah."

Deedee waited a moment and then walked around their plastic, green tree, all decorated with twinkling bulbs and silly ornaments collected over the years. She touched one, a shiny, glass pickle. "Remember when we went camping, and your dad tossed a pickle in the air, and it landed in a tree?"

"Yep," Patrick answered.

"This ornament is a memory of that time." She pulled another ornament off the tree and placed it in a different spot for a better view. "This one was your first Christmas, Santa on a train."

"I don't remember my baby Christmases," Patrick replied.

"Next year, we'll add a new one, a pink one," Deedee hinted.

"I don't really like that color, Mom. But if you want to, that's okay, I guess."

"Not for you, son. For your baby sister," Deedee said, grinning brightly.

"He's a baby girl? I mean, I just thought I'd have a brother. You're going to have a girl?" Patrick shouted, not sure if he felt happy or disappointed.

"We found out yesterday," his mom announced.

"Wow!" Patrick exclaimed. "Mom, I'm happy about that."

Deedee seemed relieved.

Patrick stood up and inspected all of the little ornaments,

asking his mom about each one. A whole set of figurines from Rudolph the Red-Nosed Reindeer had been placed here and there. He noticed nothing religious about any of the ornaments. There was no baby Jesus or nativity scenes. Of course, there never had been, but he still wondered about it this year.

That evening, Chad and Deedee wrapped some final gifts while Patrick laid out all of his marbles to admire them. He'd collected quite a number of them, so he had built a wooden box in which he had added sectional dividers. As he placed marbles in special spots, he recalled the old gentleman's words about his worth. Yet his thoughts traveled to what Leigh had told him about Jesus.

"Mom and Dad," Patrick spoke up, "Can we go to church this year for Christmas?"

"Why do you want to do that?" Deedee asked surprised.

"Well, Christmas is about baby Jesus, isn't it?"

"I guess so," Deedee answered. "We don't belong to any church, so I don't know. And we usually play games as a family."

"I know. Maybe we could make a choice this year to do something different," Patrick said carefully, as he didn't want to upset his mom.

"I doubt churches care if people are members or not for Christmas services," said Chad. "Sure, son. We'll find one to attend if you'd like."

"Thanks."

So they did. On Christmas Eve, Chad found a community church nearby, and the Melberry family, for their first time ever, sat amongst other churchgoers as they sang about the birth of the Savior and heard the Christmas story from a book in the Bible called Luke. Deedee seemed anxious to leave and begin family festivities, but Patrick listened carefully trying to make sense of it all. Finally, the service ended, and they drove home the long way to see the lit-up houses and yards full of Santas, reindeer, snowmen, and more. No family games this year.

As usual, Patrick awoke early and waited at the tree,

touching and investigating each gift until his parents joined him. Chad took a seat on the couch with a steaming cup of coffee while Deedee struggled with morning sickness. Eventually, after two cups of hot chocolate and cinnamon rolls, Patrick announced the beginning of gift opening. He passed them around and then one by one they took turns unwrapping their presents.

"There's one more in that envelope in the tree," Chad said.

Patrick read the letter from his mom and dad. He glanced at them a time or two, then set it down. He felt like crying. He knew they expected him to rejoice, but he was torn.

"Well?" Deedee waited in anticipation.

Chad recognized the conflict in Patrick's face. "What's wrong?"

"Do we have enough money for two trips this summer?" Patrick asked, heavily.

"Two? This is a trip to Texas to see Curtis. What else did you have in mind?" Chad questioned him.

"I—I'm hoping to go back to New Jersey for the National Marbles Tournament again."

"We didn't know, son. You didn't say anything, and you haven't really practiced," said Chad. He looked at Deedee who shook her head.

"To be honest, we *do* have the finances for two trips, but I'm only able to take one week of vacation," explained Chad. "Your mom won't be able to travel this summer with a newborn baby. I'm afraid you'll have to choose."

What should've been the most exciting gift of all time, turned into a dilemma. The scales leaned toward seeing Curtis, but each day, tiny weights were added to the Wildwood side, balancing the scale. The way in which Patrick had been so easily accepted, his friend Troy from Tennessee who had kept in touch all these months, another chance to make it to the semi-finals, the rides, the atmosphere—Patrick couldn't decide. He longed to see Curtis, to be with him like old times, to wrestle and ride bikes and to play pranks. But those were in the past—things wouldn't be the same ever again.

"Dad," Patrick asked, a few weeks later, "Does Curtis already know about this trip to Texas?"

"No, we haven't spoken to his dad, yet."

"Well, I've decided to go to nationals again if I can qualify," Patrick said. The guilt welled up in him as he spoke those words. If Curtis knew he chose marbles over his best friend, his heart might break again. Both their hearts would break.

"No Curtis then?" his dad asked.

Patrick tried to redeem himself. "Curtis is still my best friend, but he's gone, and when I see him and have to say goodbye, it hurts too much. And, Dad, I want to do something for myself for once, without Curtis. I want to see if *I'm* somebody more than who we used to be when we were together."

"I understand. That makes me happy, Patrick. I think maybe you're starting to grow up," his dad said.

The first day of the second semester was a gut punch for Patrick, literally. The bell rang for students to head to first period classes. His schedule had changed so that he no longer had PE, and his choir class was in an outbuilding. As he neared the exit door, he wasn't paying attention and walked into the worst person he could've bothered that morning. TJ Maloney was angry. Perhaps he'd held in all the negative words he'd wanted to pour out on Patrick the first semester, or maybe he simply felt unhappy about his schedule change. Who knows?

"You Pig!" TJ exploded. "You fill up the entire doorway!"

Carlos caught up to the two of them in seconds. "So, Fat Fart! Yeah, we remember that speaker in fifth grade when you stunk up the room. Fat Fart! You're a worthless blimp of blubber."

"Leave me alone," Patrick said trying to push his way past them.

TJ planted his feet firmly in the doorway. Carlos, who had suffered the near suffocation, or so they called it, wanted revenge.

"You're not going anywhere, Blimp," Carlos said. "Try, I dare you!"

Patrick looked around for a teacher or anyone, actually, but most students had either made it to class or ignored the threats taking place. "Get out of my way!" he said raising his voice.

"Not this time," TJ warned. "Go ahead, Carlos."

Before Patrick knew what hit him, he gasped for breath. Doubling over in excruciating pain, he saw out of the corner of his eye four feet running away from the door and heard shouts of victory in the air. He wanted to puke, he wanted to cry, he wanted to make them pay. He did none of that. Instead, Patrick snatched up his schedule that fell from his hand after the punch to his belly and holding his aching gut headed toward class.

Surprised that choir class was comprised of students from different grades, he recognized an eighth grade boy from Marbles Club, one of Leigh's friends. The guy welcomed him to the bench he occupied. Also in the class was Lissy. She waved at him from across the room. Nervous giggles rose from sections of the room as the teacher explained that each student would sing several notes in front of the class to determine in which section of the choir they'd be placed.

"Do you like to sing?" the boy from marbles asked Patrick.

"I don't know. I've never thought about it. How about you?"

"Oh, I'm terrible, but this was the only class that fit my schedule," he answered, laughing.

Sure enough, when the boy let out a few notes, he sounded like a rooster with a sore throat. Muffled giggles escaped the mouths of some students. The teacher had him sing in a deeper tone. This time he managed to hit the correct notes, but they sounded like he was gargling mouthwash.

"Patrick Melberry," the instructor said, "Welcome to choir. Please try to repeat the notes I sing." She sounded lovely as her alto voice filled the air.

Shocked, Patrick copied her song nearly perfect. He hadn't been sure if that music really left his mouth or if a stand-in sung behind him somewhere.

"Nice," she said. "Try this." The notes seemed to rise and fall like a cliff swallow darting to and fro. Again, Patrick matched her tune. He saw a few students clapping silently for him. Then his teacher asked him to move to the green bench in the middle of the three rows. Lissy had been placed there as well. She had a soft, gentle voice that sounded like hushing lullabies.

After class, Lissy stopped Patrick before he left. "Patrick, I didn't know you could sing."

"Neither did I," he said. Still somewhat surprised at his newfound ability, he kept an eye out for the bullies as he traveled to his next class. Patrick hoped that Ben wouldn't be in it.

He wasn't. Grateful, Patrick sat in the back of the room at first, then for some odd reason that he couldn't explain, he moved up three rows near the front. Instead of slumping, he paid attention to the teacher and even took notes. Even more astonishingly, he asked to eat lunch with a boy he didn't know. The kid stared at him blankly and then agreed to let Patrick join him. They discussed Christmas gifts, and it seemed the boy enjoyed video games and nothing else.

Patrick spent the rest of lunchtime playing with soap in the bathroom, wondering why he was acting so strange. "What's up with you?" he asked himself in the mirror making sure no one else was in the place. He made bubbles in his palms.

"I don't know. What's up with you?" questioned the mirror self.

"Nothing," said Patrick.

The mirror replied, "Then, why did you ask?"

"Because you're acting weird. Since when do you sing and pay attention in class?" Patrick said.

"Since you got punched in the gut," the mirror declared.

Patrick agreed. He should've smacked Carlos right back and flung him to the ground like last time. He should've, but he didn't. "Why?" he said, staring at himself in the mirror and waiting for an answer.

Finally, the reflection stated quite clearly, "You're changing, that's why!"

Patrick washed the soap from his hands, wiped them dry, and meandered through the hall to his next class.

CHAPTER 22
LISSY'S BIRTHDAY PARTY

Students in Patrick's choir section kept making remarks about his excellent voice until he started feeling uncomfortable. No one had ever built him up this way. Yes, kids in Marbles Club gave him compliments, and those were sincere, but these people made him feel as if he had a future in singing.

"Patrick, you should try out for the spring production," one girl suggested.

"Have you thought about becoming a professional vocalist?" another asked.

One of the guys that sang bass added, "We could harmonize if we practiced together."

No one called him fat or obese or Pig Boy to his face. Patrick had grown taller but hadn't lost much weight during sixth grade. So that hadn't changed. *It must be something else*, he contemplated, *that has made me different.* As he pondered the reasons, he feared that when Curtis left, he took Patrick's old self with him. *Na, that's not it.* Maybe, he thought, there was some kind of charm in those marbles that old man gave him. Perhaps, when he and his family went to church on Christmas Eve, an angel touched him and changed him.

I'll ask Leigh what he thinks, Patrick finally decided.

When he arrived in Leigh's garage, he saw pieces of paper taped everywhere. Each listed types of shots and percentages. "What's this all about?" he asked Leigh, forgetting his intention to discuss how he'd changed recently.

"Hey, Patrick! The sheets of paper over there show my percentages at tap shots. They're all in the seventy and eighty percentiles. Those over there are distance, break shots, and ride-ins, and they don't look so good."

"Oh, I see. Do you practice when I'm not here?"

"Yes! Every day for about an hour each day. I'm going to start practicing two or more hours from now on," Leigh said. "Man, I wish you could hang with me to keep me focused."

"I told my parents that I'm going to nationals this summer. So I need to practice more too. Maybe I can come over more often," said Patrick.

"That'd be great!" Leigh said, setting up the rack and lining up for a break shot. Then he moved over. "You go first," he said.

Patrick flicked his green aggie a few times and shot at the thirteen marbles sending dubs out of the ring. His shooter rolled out as well. "Would you make me some of those percentage papers?"

"Sure."

The mibsters shot for two hours that afternoon, until Deedee showed up to gather Patrick. She felt better now that his baby sister had started kicking around inside her. And now that she wasn't sick, his mom took over most of his transportation again.

"Mom, in order for me to have a chance at nationals again, I need to practice almost every day. Leigh asked if I could hang here after school more often," Patrick said this in front of Leigh hoping to manipulate her answer a bit.

"I'll see what your dad says," she answered as usual.

In the car, Patrick's mom handed him a card. "Looks like a girl's handwriting," she said.

Sure enough, the address was printed with fancy curlicues. Patrick opened it and gasped. "Mom, I'm invited to Lissy's fourteenth birthday party at the indoor city pool."

"Wow! That's the first invitation beside Curtis's you've received," his mom remarked. Realizing the hurtful nature of her statement, she added, "And it's from a girl! Congratulations!"

"Mom!"

"What shall we get her for a gift?" she asked.

"I don't know. What do girls like?" He immediately realized he shouldn't have asked because his mom immediately planned a shopping date for the two of them.

Going to the mall made Patrick feel uneasy. There were too many stores and too many people. To make matters worse, middle school girls hung out at the mall, all gathered in their little cliques and always whispering and giggling about something. *Probably talking about boys*, he thought. And the boys traveled in pairs keeping an eye out for the cute girls who tended to crowd around the coffee shops drinking sweet lattes or something of the sort.

"Mom, I don't like this place. We could just go to Walmart or something. Even the grocery store would be better than this."

"Patrick, there's quality stores here with some nice discounts today now that the holiday season is over. I think we'll find a variety of items to choose from that are on sale," Deedee said. She actually seemed chipper and much like her old self before all the morning sickness, somewhat to Patrick's dismay. He had hoped she'd given up on all the fashion, makeup and gym workouts.

"Yeah, okay, I guess."

An hour later, they were still empty handed, and Patrick's feet were sore and sweaty from his new Christmas sneakers. He never liked new shoes. They were too obvious, and it bothered him that people would say, "Hey, you got new shoes!" *No duh*, he'd think.

"Oh, great!" Patrick complained. "Ben is here." In a store across the way, Ben and another kid from school were spraying each other with cologne and gagging at the smells. Then, they laughed and tried to sneak up on a stranger to do the same. Patrick thought about Curtis and how that's something they'd do together, and he felt sad. He grabbed his mom's elbow and led her quickly into a music store.

"Does Lissy like a certain band or group?" Deedee asked.

Patrick was fed up with shopping. "Yes, she likes this music," he said, plucking a random CD from a rack. "Here, let's get this and go home," Patrick responded hastily.

Deedee turned the disc over and read, "Soundtrack to the award-winning film *The Titanic*." She hummed a tune like she knew a song. "Hmm, okay. What else would she like?"

Patrick sighed in desperation. "We have to buy two gifts?" he asked.

"Well, I have a gift bag at home, and it's too large for this small item. It would look nicer if it was filled," Deedee said.

Patrick couldn't believe it. The present *had* to fit the bag? He searched the store and saw nothing else. "Well, then" he asked, "What else is there?"

Deedee purchased the music, and they stepped out into the throng of post-holiday shoppers. Patrick stepped on someone's toes and heard a shriek, but it faded with the movement of people. He wanted to escape the mall, but his mom spied a sale in an infant and children's' clothing store.

"Oh, I just want to take a peek, Patrick—for your baby sister," Deedee pleaded. Without waiting for his response, she moseyed inside and commenced touching every miniature, baby girl item she set her eyes upon.

"Good grief!" Patrick groaned. He leaned against a rack of stuffed animals and felt his torso shifting as it swiveled and tipped. He and the rack toppled to the floor, sending furry creatures flying.

"Oh, my goodness!" a young woman hollered.

Like a whirlwind, Deedee turned around and screamed "Patty-cake!" and quickly covered her mouth as if she'd said a bad word.

"I—I found the one I wanted!" He stammered. He seized hold of the most substantial stuffed toy within reach. "It—it was on the top of the rack, and when I reached for it, this whole thing tipped over."

A store employee accepted his explanation without question, and offered to help Patrick up. Humiliated and more than anxious to depart, he pulled himself up along with the squishy animal. A plush, blue and gray dolphin with shiny black eyes smiled up at Deedee. Patrick shrugged.

His mom repeatedly apologized, then feeling the need to dismiss themselves from the store, she speedily slid her credit card at the register. The dolphin, Patrick, and Deedee exited just as swiftly.

The two weeks passed rapidly. Patrick and Leigh had spent a good deal of time practicing in his garage. Leigh's percentages kept rising while Patrick's seemed stuck at fifty percent on every shot. At least, his parents had allowed him two extra days off of endless homework. The breaks had actually improved his attitude, and his grades improved slightly.

"Leigh, have I changed since you've met me?" Patrick asked randomly.

"In what way?"

"In any way," Patrick said.

"Yes. Your marbles shooting is tons better!" Leigh answered.

"Anything else?"

"I think you've lost some weight. Why're you wanting to know? Do *you* think you've changed?" Leigh wondered.

"Um, yeah, I guess. I think I don't get as mad at people as I used to. And maybe, I'm more than just a huge kid."

"Well, then, I suppose my prayers are being answered," Leigh said grinning widely.

"You pray for *me*?" Patrick was flabbergasted.

"Yes!" Leigh punched Patrick's shoulder lightly. "Let's work on distance shots today."

And they did, for two hours straight, until Patrick's pants grew holes. In two days, he'd wear a swimsuit with skinned knees and pray that no one would make fun of his size. Maybe they'd treat him like the kids at nationals—just one of the gang.

Deedee was pleasantly pleased with how nicely Lissy's presents filled the gift bag. She insisted that Patrick write a birthday wish on the card she had selected. It had flowers and hearts on it.

"Mom, this looks like a Valentine's Day card. Couldn't you find any that had a goofy dog on the front and Happy Birthday on the inside?"

"This is a sweet one, and it does have a birthday wish inside," his mom declared. "Patrick, at least, sign your name."

When they arrived, Deedee dropped him off where a few other partygoers had gathered near the entrance. The air was chilly and a bit blustery, so they all pushed their way inside to the foyer. Patrick recognized one boy from Marbles Club and inched his way to him.

"Hi," Patrick said.

"Hey, Patrick! Good to see you," the guy replied.

To Patrick's relief Leigh showed up next. He'd stick close to Leigh during the party, he decided. Soon enough, the pool water splashed wildly as a handful of young teenagers attempted to drown one another playfully. Patrick felt more secure with his body in the water than out, so he remained splashing after others climbed out to dry off.

"Patrick," Lissy's mom called. "We're going to open gifts and then have some cake."

The party had shifted toward the deeper end of the pool where the tables had been set. Some of the other families had brought younger siblings, so as Patrick pulled himself through the water to the steps, he begged a youngster to hand him his towel. The little boy obliged, and Patrick immediately wrapped it around his torso and moved over to the group.

He felt so much heavier out of the pool. *Amazing how water can take the weight off*, he thought. He took a chair near Leigh and watched Lissy open her gifts. When she grabbed his present, he flinched. He had forgotten what it was.

"Oh, it's adorable!" Lissy squeezed the dolphin, then pulled out the Titanic disc. Puzzled, she handed it to her mom. The adults present seemed to recognize it right off.

"Lissy," her mom said. "It's a movie about a sinking ocean liner." She went on to explain some of the details which intrigued the group.

After cake, they decided to re-enact the submerging ship pretending that the pool deck collided with the iceberg, and they were all thrown into the freezing water. A few children's floaties served as the lifeboats, and only three people were allowed to hang onto each life raft. Those not able to grab hold had to dive to the bottom of the deep end.

Patrick couldn't recall learning to swim in his younger years, but he felt sure that he'd been exposed to some part of it, because he remembered how to hold his breath, flutter kick and float just a little. He panicked at the thought of not reaching a lifeboat and having to swim to the drain twelve feet below.

One parent held tight to the three float tubes, then tossed them out one by one. Immediately after that, Lissy's dad cried out, "Iceberg!" cueing them to fall into the deep end and make for one of the boats.

Patrick's adrenaline kicked in as he rapidly dog paddled to a green tube, reaching it the same time as two other kids. "Whew!" he exhaled. Further out in "the ocean," five people swam with all their might seeing that the other life raft held three survivors. Patrick watched as the last two realized their demise and abruptly dove down to the depths where the drain welcomed them.

"This game is great!" Leigh yelled. "Let's go again."

Oh, no, Patrick thought. He'd gotten lucky once. Would it happen again?

The "lifeboats" flew high and far this time. "Iceberg!" the voice bellowed.

Not a chance, Patrick feared. Everyone swam stronger and faster than he did. He'd have to dive along with Lissy, who missed out on a tube. If he had to make it to the bottom, he might seriously drown. She treaded water for a moment, then ducked under the surface gliding like a dolphin into the deep.

Patrick began to sink. It appeared to the others that he intended to descend feet first, except that his arms flailed wildly trying to rise above the surface. Swallowing water, he lost control of his body. His mind raced with thoughts of people being swallowed up in the freezing Atlantic Ocean with an enormous sinking ship in their midst. He was one of them. He would die in the deep end of the city pool at Lissy's fourteenth birthday party. This was it. The end.

Suddenly strong arms seized hold of his left shoulder and neck. Patrick grappled with the rescuer attempting to gain access to air. With haste, the lifeguard pulled his nearly weightless body to the pool's edge where many hands dragged him onto the deck.

"Patrick!" Lissy's mom shouted.

He coughed up water from his lungs, rolled onto his belly, and gagged. Thankfully, he didn't vomit, but he felt sickeningly water-logged inside and out. The entire party of guests and families surrounded him. He heard a man's voice, probably Lissy's dad, say, "Game over! Find something else to play."

Astonishingly, Patrick made a few new friends that day. His courageous attempt at drowning and then returning to life again became the talk of the party. They laughed about it later. Everyone acknowledged his bravery and humble reaction to his near-death experience.

CHAPTER 23
A NEW BABY GIRL

Curtis received a phone for Christmas, and although his calls and texts were limited, he and Patrick talked weekly.

"Maybe you're not so far away after all," Patrick told him. "At least we get to talk and laugh again."

"True, but it's not the same. My new friends aren't like you, Patrick. I can't joke around and play pranks with them because we got caught once and now they're afraid. You were never a pansy, Patrick."

Considering this, he said, "I never thought of myself as a pansy before. And I was never afraid because you were always with me, Curtis."

"Yeah, I guess so. My dad says I need to act more like a young man now that Mom isn't here. I think he just wants me to do more chores," grunted Curtis.

Patrick stuttered, "I—I think I'm changing too."

"How's that?"

"I haven't really wanted to prank anyone lately," Patrick said.

He heard Curtis gasp. "And after Carlos punched me in the gut and I didn't react, they try even harder to get under my skin."

"You should've beat the daylights out of them."

"Oh, I wanted to. Lately, though, it's easier for me to ignore them. And guess what?" Patrick asked.

"What?"

"They're punks and bullies, but I don't hate them anymore," said Patrick.

"Ha ha, I don't believe you for a second. But that's okay. Maybe you ought to come stay here and be a young man for my dad's sake, and I'll go there and whip TJ and his creepers into shape."

Patrick gave up. Curtis was being himself. "Hey, I can feel my baby sister kick through my mom's stomach."

"That's cool! When is she going to be born?" Curtis asked.

"Mom says the due date is May twenty-first."

"What's her name going to be?"

"I don't know yet," Patrick answered.

"Well, I'm going to call her Pickles," Curtis responded.

"That's weird," Patrick said laughing. It felt good to talk to Curtis. At least he told his best friend how he'd changed and was happy to have that off his chest. He knew that Curtis would be his friend forever, no matter what.

Later, Patrick shared his baby sister's nickname with his parents. Chad held back his grin for fear that Deedee would come unglued. She shook her head in disapproval and left the room.

"Dad, what name will she have?" Patrick asked.

"We haven't decided. Besides Pickles, what would you suggest?"

"You're asking me?" Up until this point Patrick saw this new baby situation as something his parents would deal with, and he'd be the onlooker big brother.

"Of course! You need to call her something when you change her diapers," his dad said with a chuckle.

"Gross! No way, Dad!" At that, Patrick decided that if he referred to her as Pickles, he'd never be required to do anything with her poop and pee.

His dad changed the subject. "Son, since I assume you'll qualify for the National Marbles Tournament, and since your mom can't chaperone you with a new baby, I've already asked my boss for the week off."

"You're going to Wildwood!?" Patrick exploded. "We're going to have so much fun! I can't wait!"

"So I'm giving you permission to practice with Leigh five days a week, providing you keep your grades the way they are," his dad explained.

Patrick's effort had improved, bringing his poor grades to average ones. He wanted to make his dad proud of him, so he intended to practice hard and raise his grades even higher. *I am growing up*, he thought.

Sixth grade started rough, but the end of the year proved to be rewarding. Patrick had been selected to sing a solo in the final choir concert, and Leigh encouraged him to perform for him every day they practiced. He taught him a couple of worship songs, and to Patrick's surprise, he enjoyed praise music. He still didn't understand the whole Jesus message and forgiveness and all, but he *did* believe that Jesus was real and listened to people's prayers.

"Every time, I get a stick, you have to sing your performance song," Leigh said.

"That's funny," Patrick said. "I'll lose my voice. You get sticks all the time."

"Hmm, okay then," Leigh said. "When I run the rack, you have to sing."

"What's running the rack?"

"Thirteen marbles make a rack, and when I shoot all of them out of the ring without missing, it's called running the rack."

"I've never seen anyone run the rack. That would be incredible, Leigh!"

That spring brought more rain than usual; however, Leigh and Patrick practiced consistently no matter the weather. Today, during their practice, the rings in the city park were wet. Instead of playing the traditional six-inning games, they took turns shooting till they missed. Leigh got close to running the rack but couldn't get past the eleventh marble two times in a row. The intensity of his concentration was impressive.

Patrick appreciated the dampness. His shooter stuck better when the ring was wet. He set up the rack, selected a great angle for the break, and flicked with spin. He launched his green aggie a couple of inches in the air to avoid losing aim and power in the slight puddles that had formed here and there.

"Wow!" Leigh exclaimed. "Great shot!"

Patrick's agate spun like a whirlwind in the center of the ring right beside two mibs. The marble he knocked out flew away, hitting the wooden platform barrier and bounced into the leaves and dirt. Leigh picked it up and wiped it off. Patrick held his shooter precisely as needed to hit the tap shot and keep his agate in the middle of the pack of marbles.

Click and zip! The second mib whizzed out of the ring, leaving his shooter spinning and ready to knock out the next three marbles, one after the other. A total of five—Patrick had never run more than four marbles before.

Leigh held his breath in anticipation, and he prayed.

Patrick felt confident that he'd hit the next marble as it was a short, three-inch shot, yet the other marbles had scattered some during play. He smacked it. The mib rolled out, and the green aggie appeared to be doing the same.

"Stay, stay, stay!" Patrick shouted. He tracked his shooter to the edge of the ring where it slowed to a stop in a strip of water. "It's in!"

Leigh jumped with excitement. "Get a stick, Patrick!"

Patrick sized up the arrangement of mibs in the circle. Every marble was clearly a distance shot. He was still fifty-fifty on long shots, and his nerves were causing him some anxiety.

"Pick the best angle, Patrick, not the closest marble," Leigh suggested.

Patrick knew Leigh was right. If he played more like Leigh, he'd have a higher chance of hitting the closer marble, but in this case, it was a risk. Instead, he aimed at a mib with a backup just behind it and to the side. Wiping the moisture from his fingers and his agate, he focused on an imaginary line between his shooter and the two mibs. He flicked with confidence releasing the green sphere in deliberate determination that it would strike its mark.

Smack! Thwack! The shooter slammed into one marble, which picked up momentum creating a chain reaction. The first mib spun sidewise slamming into the backup marble causing both to exit the ring simultaneously.

"Dubs!" Leigh yelled. "Patrick! You got your first stick!" He jumped up and down in exhilaration.

Patrick felt it. The incredible satisfaction of reaching the goal—like summiting a mountain that seemed impossible to climb. It was the culmination of practice, persistence, and a positive attitude. It was his to experience. He grinned from ear to ear.

So, Leigh, how about *you* sing my choir performance piece to *me*?" Patrick asked.

"You got it!" Leigh rasped out the song creating an utter cacophony.

Patrick took in the scene with all his heart. Leigh's friendship filled the black hole that Curtis had left behind. And it felt safe and secure.

That evening, Patrick's parents celebrated the stick by taking Patrick out to his favorite restaurant. They discussed the qualifying tournament, New Jersey, the coming of his baby sister, and the end of sixth grade. For the first time in what seemed like forever, Patrick felt hope and happiness.

The choir concert approached rapidly, and Patrick found himself singing in the mirror, wearing a button-up shirt and a tie. "I can't breathe with this thing around my neck!" he complained.

"Just for tonight. Then you can rip it off," his dad said, chuckling.

"No, Patrick. You may unhook it and pull it off gently," said his mother.

"Ugh!" It had taken up all of his courage to perform in front of a huge audience, but to sport this suit, he'd need a double portion of bravery and two scoops of chocolate ice cream.

They arrived in the gymnasium. His parents took seats up front, and Patrick scooted away into the choir room. He was almost as nervous as his first day at the National Marbles Tournament. At least the restroom was nearby. Finally, they filed out and onto the risers, taking their assigned places. Patrick's knees shook as he stood anxiously awaiting his solo. He wished it was first, so he could get it over with.

Why did I let them convince me to do this? he thought as the choir sang several songs.

"Next, Patrick Melberry will perform a wonderful piece for all of you," his teacher announced.

He swallowed, licked his lips, hooked his fingers behind his back to prevent from shaking. Then the pianist struck a few notes, and he began. Staring over the heads of the audience, Patrick allowed his voice to carry louder and with impressive volume as he grasped for the higher notes. Eventually, his throat relaxed, and the tune hushed to a hum. Patrick bowed to a roaring applause before he turned and made his way back to his space. Afterward, classmates swarmed around congratulating him on his splendid performance, as did their parents.

"Thanks, thanks," he answered. He felt humbled, and uncomfortable, wanting more than anything to get out of his stuffy clothes.

If Deedee had had a smaller watermelon sagging from her belly, she'd have wanted to stay and soak in the glory, but she hugged Patrick instead. "That was the most beautiful song I've ever heard!" she said, smiling proudly. "However, I need to rest my back after sitting straight for so long."

Chad winked, so Patrick grasped the tie and jerked it from his collar. Tossing it carelessly into the air, he sent it to its fate somewhere in the mass of mingling people.

May seventeenth arrived. Mrs. Lee called out opponents' names in the qualifying tournament. Patrick had been paired with Leigh in the first match. Remembering sportsmanship above all else, they shook hands, shared encouragement, and racked the marbles. Leigh beat Patrick both games but not without tough competition. In one game, they had gotten down to the last marble, each holding six points apiece.

Patrick missed. Leigh missed. Patrick missed again. Leigh moved to a less obvious place around the circle to aim. It seemed further away. He took his time, then flicked his aggie rolling straight in line with the last mib. It struck dead on, and Leigh won.

When they shook hands, Leigh whispered, "Never shoot at the same marble more than twice from the same spot. It's a lesson Mrs. Lee taught me."

The tournament ended in the heat of the day. Leigh and Patrick qualified as did Lissy, who won the girls' league undefeated. The news reporters commenced their interviews and photographs until Chad interrupted, claiming that Deedee needed some air-conditioning and to conclude the celebration quickly. Patrick noticed his mom panting as if she might pass out, so he left the hubbub whereas his dad hurried him along to the car. Carrying his trophy on his lap, Chad made a beeline to the center of town, the hospital.

"What's happening?" Patrick asked anxiously.

"Your mom has gone into labor, Patrick. Looks like your sister is about to enter the world!"

"Now?" Patrick asked as they pulled up to the emergency entrance and watched his mom being pushed into the maternity ward in a wheelchair. She was squirming around as if she felt considerably uncomfortable. Chad ran alongside the wheelchair and motioned for Patrick to hurry up. They rushed into a room where Patrick was immediately dismissed. A nurse asked him to stay in the nearby waiting area.

Patrick prayed aloud, "God, please help my mom deliver this baby quickly."

God answered expediently. A nurse overheard his prayer and said, "Any minute now, big brother!" As she darted into his mom's room, he caught a brief glimpse of commotion.

Not more than fifteen minutes later, Chad entered the waiting area with face beaming and eyes sparkling. "Your sister is here!"

"Is—is Mom okay?" Patrick felt exhilaration and distress at the same time.

"She's doing exceptionally well," his dad responded, wrapping his arms around Patrick. "Come-on, let's go back into the room and see her."

Minutes later, Patrick laid eyes on the most beautiful little person he'd ever seen. The tiny, swaddled bundle, the size of the plush dolphin he'd given Lissy, lay sweetly in the arms of his father, who spoke gently to her. Then, he motioned for Patrick to sit down in the vinyl-covered chair where he proceeded to hand over the newborn to her big brother.

"Dad, I'm scared," Patrick said. "I don't know how to hold her."

"Firmly and carefully," Chad answered. "Like this." He placed her in Patrick's cradled arms.

Patrick stared at every minute detail of her cute, tiny face. A wisp of black hair stuck out from under a snug pink wrap on her head. He touched it gently. She wiggled and let out a tiny peep, then pursed her lips for a second. Patrick leaned in and kissed her forehead ever so sweetly and gently. "I love you," he said.

"We named her Tiffany!" Chad stated proudly.

"Tiff," Patrick repeated.

Chad almost corrected him but held his tongue.

"You look like a Tiff," Patrick said peering into her slightly open eyes. She wriggled a bit more and squeaked out a squall that increased in intensity. "What do I do, Dad?"

"Babies cry; don't worry. Try holding her upright on your chest," his dad suggested, careful not to interrupt their developing bond.

Patrick wrapped both hands around her bundled body, turned her head onto his shoulder, and immediately Tiffany burped out a bubble of air. Then she relaxed. Patrick's entire body flushed with adoration. "I love her so much, Dad!"

Patrick looked at his mom resting in the bed and decided she looked beautiful—tousled hair, no make-up, just an overjoyed smile upon her face. She reached for Tiffany, although Patrick hesitated to give her up. He didn't see how he could spend a minute without her close to him, so he scooted as near to his mom's bed as possible. The Melberry family was a picturesque scene of happiness and contentment, of delight and fulfillment.

After a long day and night in the hospital room, the Melberry's were anxious to leave as no one could sleep with all the in and out of hospital professionals, lights blinking, and the occasional beeping from the nurse's station. Baby Tiffany, however, hardly let out even a whimper of dissatisfaction other than several squeaky sounds followed by a low-pitched screech when she was hungry.

"Tiffany Pickles," Patrick said under his breath in the middle of that night. As hard as it was to admit that Curtis was right, his baby sister's whimpers sounded more like the squeak of a pickle being bitten into—that noise as it scrapes against teeth like a piece of twisting rubber. Then crunch, a tasty pickle. *What a name!*

CHAPTER 24

SPORTSMANSHIP

Patrick forced himself to hand Tiffany over to his mom just as he and his dad entered the airport security line. He'd spent his days practicing marbles and holding his sister and nearly nothing else.

"Coo," a noise escaped Tiffany's lips. Patrick felt sure she told him to have a safe trip, play great marbles, say hi to Troy, bring a trophy back, don't get a sunburn, and play in the ocean, all for her. Then, come home quickly so they could look into each other's eyes again and again.

"Okay, Tiff! I will!" Patrick said agreeing with her. Then he tore his eyes from his baby sister, and he and his dad made their way through security.

On the plane Chad let out a sigh. "Patrick, I haven't been on a vacation in a very long time. I'm looking forward to this time together with you, my son."

"Me too, Dad. I just wish we didn't have to be away from Mom and Tiff for so long," Patrick said.

"Then let's have a fantastic time, so you'll have a tremendous story to tell them when we return!"

"Yep, for sure!"

Groggy from a delayed flight due to stormy weather, Patrick sloshed through a puddle exiting the shuttle to the car rental. His dad would drive to Wildwood this year. The rain pelted the glass as streams of water coursed down the windows making it hard to see. The precipitation fell quicker than the wipers could swish it away, but Chad steered expertly through Philadelphia, across the bridge, and south into New Jersey.

A couple hours later his dad said, "We're near Wildwood, Patrick," waking him up.

Patrick looked for the amusement park rides and tall hotels lining the beach, but the clouds hung low releasing their moisture. "How can you tell?" he asked.

"Well, I think I saw a highway sign just a bit ago. Besides, GPS told me."

"Who? Oh, never mind." Patrick rubbed his eyes and blinked the sleepiness from his brain.

When they arrived at the hotel, Patrick noticed people huddling under the parking garage or braving the rain and wind, holding firmly to whipping umbrellas. "Dad, did we bring umbrellas?"

"No, but we have those old plastic ponchos that your mom sent with us," his dad answered. "Patrick, will the officials hold the tournament in the rain?"

"Yes, I think so," Patrick answered, wondering about that himself.

They darted into the lobby with their luggage. Standing there dripping from the shower, Patrick recognized a few committee members, yet, he forgot their names. Nonetheless, he shook hands and introduced his dad to them. Chad returned the gestures, gathered their meal tickets and room keys, then proceeded to enter the elevator.

"Let's walk up the stairs," Patrick suggested, feeling like he'd been sluggish for hours and needed some exercise.

"Okay, but that's six floors, son," Chad said, shrugging his shoulders.

Reaching the third floor, Patrick changed his mind. "Uh, let's catch the elevator here."

"By the end of the week, we'll likely run all the way up those steps, Patrick," his dad said, chortling.

"Ha! I'd like to see you do that, Dad!"

Room six-hundred seven would accommodate Patrick and his dad for the coming week. Opening the door, memories flooded his mind—sandy floors, sweet treats in the miniature refrigerator, hanging out on the balcony, and staring in awe at the boardwalk in lights and the mibsters. He thought about all his friends that he could hardly wait to meet again.

Ring, ring. Patrick's phone buzzed. "It's Troy!" he said and then pushed the green button. The voice on the other end exploded in excitement.

"We just got here! What room are you in?" Troy shouted.

It seemed only seconds before the two of them slapped high-fives as if a year never passed at all. They chattered nonstop until another knock on the door. It was Leigh and Alejandro. Soon, the room filled with Lissy and Rosia and their parents, as well as Mr. Jerry. The reunion lasted but a short time as the tournament banquet was about to begin.

Patrick felt at home, respected and accepted as he and his dad and the Colorado crew filed into the dining room. He knew what to expect and walked cheerfully across the stage when introduced, receiving his shirt and schedule for the preliminaries. The committee discussed rules, including how they would handle wind-action and rain. So they would shoot in a drizzle on wet, sandy rings.

The next morning, Leigh gathered the team together for prayer. Mrs. Lee huddled with them under the boardwalk as the mist tried to make up its mind if it would rise or smother them.

"Did we pray before the tournament last year?" Patrick asked.

"You were so nervous, you didn't know what happened," Alejandro said, laughing.

"Oh," Patrick replied.

Mrs. Lee's beach tent sat in the sand next to a concrete pillar under the wooden planks of the boardwalk. "Be careful not to whack your heads on the slabs," she warned. Then, she slipped a rain jacket over her head and popped open her umbrella. She had volunteered to referee on the first day.

The games commenced as players wiped the rain from their shooters and fingers, then knuckled down on the rings. Astonishingly, within minutes of play, the announcer called out the first stick of the tournament going to Leigh from Colorado. Patrick was elated for his friend and practice partner. The crowd hooted and applauded. He wanted to get a stick, too.

Patrick's shorts were plastered against his legs, and his tournament shirt was soaked through. His aggie stuck nicely in the ring as it struck mib after mib, but the gathering sand and sheets of rainwater prevented the marbles from rolling all the way out of the circle. He struggled with balancing backspin and power. After he finished the match, he plodded to the tent where Rosia stood out of the drizzling rain. She was weeping.

"What's the matter, Rosia?" Patrick asked.

"I haven't hit any marbles out of the ring, not one! I don't have enough power to shoot through the wet sand." She sniffed, seemingly distressed.

Patrick explained his own struggles. Then Lissy joined them and complained about her difficulties with the weather. Mr. Jerry drew near their group, listening to their grievances. Then he intervened quite boldly.

"Listen kids, a good player isn't defined by their shooting but by their attitude and sportsmanship. You're not going to help yourselves by making excuses. Everyone is shooting under the same conditions, so get out there, shakes hands, and give encouraging words. If nothing else, you'll make someone else feel better, and it might improve your game as well."

"You're right, Mr. Jerry. Thank you," Patrick replied.

Leigh finished a match earning back-to-back sticks, then proceeded to the tent to dry off. "How's it going guys?"

"Congrats on the sticks!" Patrick said, beaming.

"You like playing in the rain. How're you doing?" Leigh asked.

"I'm not used to wet *and* sandy rings," Patrick responded, but I still hope to get a stick."

"Use less backspin on the break and distance shots. Oh, and launch your aggie further into the ring so it lands closer to the pack of marbles instead of rolling into them," he told Patrick.

As it continued to rain, everyone and everything became soggier. Patrick took his shoes off as the moist sand weighted them down. He enjoyed squishing the cool sand between his toes—almost as much as playing with soap bubbles. He saw his dad huddled under the boardwalk, out of the rain, and motioned for him to come watch his games. When his dad crawled out, he smacked his head twice on the concrete abutments. Patrick had seen several people hit their heads that morning.

It's dangerous under the boardwalk! Patrick thought.

By midmorning the showers tapered off long enough for the flag-raising ceremony, the Wildwood Days song, to which Leigh and Patrick danced joyfully, and the group pictures. The referees squeegeed the rings and scraped as much sand off as possible. Suddenly, the tramcars made a racket as people moved freely along the boardwalk. Chad waited for Patrick to depart from group photos to clap him on the back and hug him for his superb attitude in the messy conditions.

"Son, I'm completely astonished at the quality of play you and some of the other mibsters have shown today. I didn't know what to expect of nationals," his dad said.

"It's sure different than last year, but I'm getting the hang of it. Thanks, Dad!"

"You're soaking wet. How're you feeling?"

"Drenched!" Patrick answered, laughing. "Not hot like last year."

Following the group photos, it started to drizzle again, and the wind picked up. Patrick managed to launch his aggie into the center of a rack of marbles and knock a mib out, but as he began to take his next shot, the referee stopped him.

"Wait! Marbles are still rolling," the referee said. "Wind action."

Sure enough, one of the other mibs that was bumped in the break looked as if it might roll out of the ring by the force of wind. Unfortunately, it came to a halt within inches of the edge. Patrick realized his opponent would select that shot when his turn arrived. He hoped to get a decent run before that happened.

"You may take your shot, now," the referee announced.

Patrick successfully knocked out two more marbles, then his aggie spun wildly in the other direction due to the wind. He immediately bent over his shooter, placing his cupped hands near the marble to block the wind. Thank goodness Mrs. Lee taught him how to cup his shooter or his turn would've ended at that point.

"Slow down, slow down," Patrick spoke to his green agate as it inched closer to the edge of the ring and the lone marble that rolled there earlier. He lifted his cupped hands, and his shooter halted. *Now what?* he thought. *Shoot at this tap shot and take a chance on missing and leaving it for his opponent or aim back into the center of the ring where a pack of marbles lay slightly scattered.*

The misty rain dampened the ring while Patrick tried to make up his mind. *Leigh would take the tap shot. No, he'd hit it like a ride-in on its side so his shooter would whip back to the center again.* He looked up. Leigh and Chad stood nearby watching intently. He knew they wouldn't cheat by signaling or cueing him in any way. He took a risk. *I'm going to try it like a ride-in,* he decided. He wiped his fingers and shooter dry, then knuckled down and flicked.

Leigh's shout let Patrick know he'd done it. The referee called out the score, "Four marbles to none. Still first inning."

His aggie nestled between to two close mibs putting Patrick's backspin to the test. *Not too much power,* he thought. He tipped his knuckles into the ring, flicked, and sent the mib flying out. His shooter rested where it had started. Again, he tipped and spun the other marble out. A gust spread over the ring, displacing a couple marbles, so the referee put them back in place and gave him permission to take his turn.

"Game marble," the referee stated. "You need one to win."

What a way to send the nerves riveting throughout his body. One marble to earn a stick! He glanced at Leigh and his dad. Lissy had joined them. She smiled as if she already knew the outcome. *Okay, I'll do it,* Patrick thought. He aimed, flicked, and hit! The wind caught hold of both his shooter and the mib as they sped swiftly out of the circle.

Lissy jumped up and down yelling, "You got a stick! You got a stick!"

Patrick snatched his agate, turned toward his opponent, shook his hand, and said, "It's your turn next. I hope you get a stick too."

"Thanks, I'll try," the boy said.

Patrick had just beat one of the top players, but in his mind, he was just a kid who loved marbles like him. A fellow mibster, a friend. Day one of preliminaries came to a close, and the sopping rags and dripping umbrellas, tents, and tarps were dumped in wagons or thrown over shoulders for the trek back to the hotel.

Mrs. Lee appeared at the Melberry's door awhile later. "May I come in?" she asked.

"Of course," Chad said, inviting her inside. "How was refereeing in the rain?"

"I had the privilege of encouraging a lot of frustrated kids," she replied. "However, I wanted to tell you how impressed I am at Patrick's good attitude today. What a fantastic sport!"

"I think so too," Chad replied.

"What about me?" Patrick asked, stepping in the room from the balcony.

"Patrick," Mrs. Lee continued. "Your superb sportsmanship caught the attention of some referees and parents watching today."

"Uh, that's good," he said. "And I got my first stick at nationals!"

"Yes, I heard it over the speakers. I'm so happy for you!" she said. Then she added, "Leigh is in first place right now according to the statistics sheet. Look."

"He is? Wow! I hope he wins!" Patrick said with great delight. He searched the day one statistics paper, found his own name in fourteenth place and noticed Alejandro in second place.

"Patrick, I believe he has a chance. Winning the national championship has been his ambition since he made it to semi-finals. You know how much he's practiced."

"Yeah, I did, too!" Patrick responded.

"Someone will earn the best sport award. Which do you think will carry the longest and most influential legacy?" she asked.

"What do you mean?"

"Which one is the most important to you?" Mrs. Lee asked.

"Oh. I guess I'd rather win and be made King of Marbles," Patrick decided.

"Very few people in the world may claim that kind of title. Their names go down in history and live forever in the National Marbles Hall of Fame," she said.

"That's so awesome! I'd like to win!" Patrick replied.

"Well, maybe you will, but if you don't, what you've learned about sportsmanship has spilled over into your life. I've seen how you've changed from an ornery, angry boy to a kind, young man."

"I certainly agree with that!" Chad added.

"Whether you win a crown and all the prizes or not, you're already making a difference to the people around you, and that's what I believe is the most important skill a person can learn from the game of marbles—sportsmanship isn't just for marbles, it's for life."

Patrick nodded. He felt more content than he had in many months, yet that yearning hope spilled out. "Then, I'd like to be a good sport for the rest of my life *and* win the National Marbles Tournament!"

Chad laughed heartily. "Oh, son! I love you!"

CHAPTER 25

MARBLES CHAMPION

The weather cleared for the rest of the week. In fact, the sun dried up all the rings, so they were smooth and slick. Patrick wrestled with his green aggie as it was larger than his other shooters and kept spinning out of the ring. With regret, he selected to use his old brown aggie, a smaller, rougher marble. With it, his backspin kicked in more easily.

"Oh well," Patrick told Leigh. "The green one got me my first stick ever, but this brown one will just have to do what I tell it to do."

"That's right!" Leigh said.

Day two of preliminaries passed successfully for Leigh and Alejandro who held their top places overall. Patrick dropped to sixteenth place. Rosia remained in the lower half of the girls' bracket, but Lissy was tied for ninth. It was boat ride day, so the crew climbed aboard and set out to sea. Chad brought with him a bag of cheese puffs. A flock of seagulls were determined to steal them, so he passed handfuls to the kids who pinched them between their fingers and lifted their arms high into the salty air.

"Yikes," a girl squealed. "It flew too close, so I dropped it." Two gulls dove for the descending treat, and one snatched it in its beak before it hit the ocean.

Leigh held his palm up and a bird flapped overhead for a second, then attacked the pile of orange puffs with great determination. It managed to scatter all but one, which it swiftly seized.

"Mom would hate this!" Patrick cried. A bird released a stream of poop across the deck as it dove in for a cheese puff.

Eventually, the captain terminated their fun as feeding seagulls was unacceptable in New Jersey. The ride did result in a pod of dolphins putting on a show off the starboard side. The gentle breeze and warm air felt inviting. Chad lay down in a lawn chair and relaxed in the bright sunshine. Troy had latched onto Patrick. The two of them were nearly inseparable the whole time. They discussed hitting the surf on Wednesday and amusement park rides on Thursday.

That evening, Chad and Patrick rode the noisy tramcar from one end of the boardwalk to the other, stepping off to play mini golf, check out the hermit crabs in cages, play in the arcades, and eat pizza covered in French fries and mustard. Patrick appreciated his dad's company more than he had his mom's the year before. Feeling guilty about that, he bought Deedee and Tiffany gifts hoping it would ease his conscience. It didn't.

Wednesday arrived with top quality shooting. Multiple sticks were announced that day, and not all of them by Leigh or Alejandro. Patrick never shot more than a run of four, but he found pleasure in each game nonetheless. The boys he played against joked with him about his nickname after someone let it slip earlier that morning. They didn't say it with malice but used it as a term of endearment as they praised him for his quality shooting.

"Hey, Pudgy Knuckles," a younger mibster called. "You have excellent backspin!"

Another boy, a quality player currently in third place said, "I've been coming to nationals for years. My family has played for as long as I can remember. The only people who get nicknames are the ones who everybody likes."

"Really?" Patrick wondered.

"Seems like it. I think Pudgy Knuckles is perfect!" he said.

Patrick's heart swelled with a sense of belonging. He began to realize that his weight didn't define him—his actions did. His words did. People enjoyed his company and sought him out for encouragement, and he gladly obliged.

After day three of preliminary play, Patrick, Chad, and Troy hiked the forever distance to the ocean from the boardwalk. That's when Patrick whispered quietly to himself, "You wouldn't be so exhausted if you lost some weight." Answering his own comment, he said, "Okay, I will. I'll try."

"What's that, son?" Chad overheard Patrick mumbling.

"Uh, I—I think we should ride bikes more often, Dad."

"No kidding. I've never seen a beach extend as long as a desert. Thank goodness, there's an enormous oasis on the other side." Chad took a breath. "Whew!"

Finally, reaching the water, they waded out reveling in the incredible power of the massive ocean. The waves slammed them, rolled them, engulfed them, and they returned for more. Finally, worn out and panting, they lay in the sand. Troy turned toward Patrick. "We're lucky we didn't make semi-finals."

"How's that lucky?" Patrick asked.

"We get to play in the ocean while they're all practicing for tomorrow."

"Yeah, I guess you're right, but I still would've liked a trophy," Patrick said.

"Not me! Let's jump in the waves one more time," Troy shouted, peeling Patrick from the sunken sand and dragging him to his feet.

Chad shook his head. "No thanks, I'm waterlogged boys."

Returning to the hotel, Patrick sat next to Leigh who was talking with Alejandro in the lobby. "We can't be in the same semi-finals league because we're kind of from the same team," Leigh explained.

"So, we could technically play against each other in finals if we win our leagues?" Alejandro asked, confirming Leigh's statement.

"Yep!"

"Wow! That'd be excellent!" Alejandro replied.

Leigh gave Patrick a friendly shove and asked, "You'll be there to cheer us both on, won't you?"

"Of course!"

Troy piped in. "I guess I have a dilemma, because the boy from Tennessee is also in semi-finals."

"We'll just need to encourage all of the players then."

Leigh nodded in agreement. "That sounds like you, Pudgy Knuckles!"

Early the next morning, Mrs. Lee took Leigh to the rings to warm up. When Patrick arrived, Leigh had already shot three sticks and was attempting to run the rack. He prepared for the eleventh marble, prayed silently, and actually hit it. Without celebrating, he moved to a new position and aimed at the twelfth mib, never having reached this far before. He hit it with such power that it bounced out of the concrete slab.

"One last marble!" Patrick screamed.

Leigh's concentration was so deep that he didn't hear Patrick. He rolled the aggie between his fingers, placed his hand squarely on the ring, and then eyed the final mib, which rested nearly two feet away.

Distance shot, Patrick thought to himself. *Last I remember, his percentage on distance shots was around eighty percent.*

Leigh released his shooter and without delay, it smacked the mib dead on, sending it out of the ring and into the wooden barrier. His agate continued to spin in place like a mini whirlwind.

Patrick couldn't contain himself. He rushed over to bear hug his friend as did Mrs. Lee and Chad. No matter what happened in semi-finals and finals today, Leigh was his champion.

Leigh ended up winning his league and would play in finals for the championship. Alejandro shot his best, but the boy from Tennessee took first in his group and would face Leigh a bit later. Patrick felt the butterflies—no not butterflies, dragon flies—whipping around in his stomach as the committee set up the finals ring. Patrick, Troy, and Chad grabbed seats nearest the ring.

Lissy sat with her parents a few seats away. Patrick could tell she'd been crying. She had lost a playoff for the final spot in the semi-finals. She had stepped off the ring into her mom's arms and remained with her.

Leigh appeared relaxed and confident. He had spent time under the boardwalk talking to Jesus before setting foot on the finals ring. Same as last year, the announcer called out each shot. Back and forth, the Tennessee boy and Leigh took turns ending most of the games with sticks. However, at the conclusion of the thirteenth game of a fifteen-game final, the score was seven games to six, with Leigh in the lead.

Patrick rubbed his hands together as the anticipation grew. Leigh had the break shot and knocked out four marbles. Then his aggie rolled out. His opponent moved in and scored six marbles before ending his turn. Seven marbles would end the game, the match, and the tournament. Leigh had to hit all the rest to win. Cameras and reporters prepared to jump into the melee if that was to happen. Patrick also intended to plow into the winning circle.

"I don't think I can handle this tension," Chad whispered to Patrick. "I had no idea this tournament would cause me so much anxiety."

"Like when mom had Tiff?" Patrick asked.

"Uh, not quite that nervous, but this is intense!" his dad said quietly.

Leigh managed to tie the game six to six leaving the final marble in the center of the ring. They each missed it twice.

Never shoot at the same marble twice from the same spot, Patrick kept repeating in his mind. *Move to a different place*, he thought trying to send brain waves to Leigh.

Leigh paced this way and that, started to take a shot from the same place. He then stood up and moved to the other side of the ring, knelt down, aimed, and fired. That was it. A new King of Marbles. Before the crowd overtook him, Patrick observed Leigh lifting his head and hands to the sky in thanks to Jesus.

Everything after that moment seemed like a blur until the kiss. The king and queen had been seated in royal thrones, adorned with crowns and numerous prizes, including a college scholarship, but the final culmination of kingship was to kiss the queen on the cheek. Patrick never considered this part of the ceremony last year, but he felt completely uncomfortable now.

"I'd kiss her," Troy told Patrick. "She's cute."

"Yuck," Patrick said. His feelings were mixed.

Leigh seemed sincerely embarrassed as he leaned toward the grinning young lady and gently pressed his lips on her cheek.

"Again!" the crowd shouted. "For the cameras!"

Leigh seriously fidgeted this time. He shook his head once and then glanced at the queen who waited patiently for the second smooch. Patrick thought of Curtis. "If my best friend was up there, he'd kiss her smack dab on the lips!" he said.

"You're probably right," his dad said.

Leigh mustered up the courage and tried again, but this time, he held the smooch for much longer until the girl pulled away red in the face. Patrick felt dizzy as if he'd done the kissing, and he was grateful when the couple were escorted off the stage. The Marble Man had previously handed Leigh a rack to sign, and he received the thirteen game marbles as well as a corked bottle full of finals ring sand.

"I need to make a stop on the way back to the hotel," Leigh told Patrick.

"Why?"

"You'll see."

Leigh headed just off the main street to an open garage filled with rental bicycles and carriages. Still wearing his crown and championship T-shirt, Leigh shook the owner's hand, talked for a bit, then the gentleman sent Leigh toward a wall. Patrick entered and noticed the wall was covered in famous people's signatures, including many of the past marbles champions. Leigh signed his name, sketching a cross next to it, then left.

Patrick remembered a tradition from last year, and he started planning the final celebration of Leigh's championship. Before they reached the hotel lobby, he spread the word to as many friends as possible. Leigh didn't make it back to his room and neither did the girl champion. A horde stood in their way, dragged them to the pool, and tossed them in with all of their clothes on. Then everyone else jumped in, even Mrs. Lee and Mr. Jerry.

"Well, Dad?" Patrick called. "Aren't you coming in?"

Chad shrugged his shoulders, then took a leaping jump onto his belly sending a spray of water in all directions, even onto the people sunbathing on the deck. The splashing and commotion went on until Leigh finally pulled himself out, leaving a trail of puddles behind him.

"Dad," Patrick said exuberantly, "I can't wait for the rides tonight."

"After the Hall of Fame, right?" his dad asked.

"Yeah," Patrick answered. "You'll like the place."

After Patrick and his dad dried off, they changed and got ready to go out for the evening. They headed to the Hall of Fame, and as they entered, Chad took time examining the years' worth of plaques, posters, and memorabilia from days gone by. He enjoyed the history. Then he motioned for Patrick to take a look at something.

"What is it, Dad?"

"This giant plaque. It lists all the national best sports of marbles," he said.

"Really? I didn't see it last time. So, sportsmanship is included in the Hall of Fame. That's cool!" Patrick said.

Patrick didn't gorge on pizza as he did the year before. *If I'm going to try to lose weight, I have to start somewhere*, he thought. And it didn't bother him to eat three pieces instead of four and drink one soda instead of two.

Feeling restless, Patrick went to the back of the room where Troy stood against the wall with his parents. The dedication of last year's king and queen was coming to a close, and the announcement of best sport was saved for last.

"You deserve it," Troy said.

"So do you," Patrick said, smiling.

A buzzing sound filled Patrick's ears. His head felt like it was under water or perhaps it was more like the thrumming inside an airplane. Either way, he didn't clearly hear the proclamation until he observed heads turning his direction. Troy shoved him.

"Why did you do that?" Patrick seemed oblivious.

"They called your name!" Troy declared.

"Mine?"

"Patrick Melberry," the speaker called again, "Chosen by the referees and this year's committee members as the boy's National Best Sport award winner!"

He moved through the crowd, stepping around kids sitting on the floor and toward the podium. Feeling numb, he took his place next to a girl from Wildwood who'd earned the girl's Best Sport award. He glanced at her, managing to speak a few audible words of congratulations. Then his eyes scanned the audience, who snapped photo after photo. They were all smiling, and many folks clapped and hollered. Chad stood up waving his hand in sheer delight.

A thought hit him like a brick. *I don't have to kiss her, do I? Did that happen last year? I don't remember!* His face turned scarlet for a moment at the thought and until he realized that he and the girl had been dismissed and everyone was free to take their leave and enjoy the boardwalk. He breathed out like a deflating balloon in relief.

"You'll receive some scholarship money for that award," Mrs. Lee said. "But I think the benefit will serve you more than any cash you'll obtain."

"Thanks," Patrick replied. Suddenly, he felt like a million dollars' worth of energy. Grabbing his dad's hand, he asserted, "Time for rides!"

Not until Morey's Piers shut down the amusement parks, turned the lights out, and started shuffling people toward the main boardwalk did Chad, Patrick, and all of his friends give up on the fun. With aching muscles and feeling exhausted, Patrick begged his dad, "Please, oh please, can we take the tramcar instead of walking all the way back?"

"I'm with you on that, son," his dad agreed.

Back at the hotel, the celebration continued on the pool deck where mibsters, parents, and committee members gathered. One giant marbles family.

The next morning, after breakfast, Chad pulled the rental car to the lobby doors where Patrick waited with all their luggage. Good-byes had been tearful, but the week had been rewarding, and Patrick intended to earn his way back next year to compete and watch Leigh be inducted into the Hall of Fame.

"Dad, before we leave, let's do one more thing," Patrick suggested.

"What's that?"

"Run up the six flights of stairs!"

"You got it!" Chad said, placing his foot on the first step and motioning for Patrick to do the same. "Go!"

Chad disappeared around the first turn on floor number one, while Patrick swiftly exited the stairwell, stepped inside the elevator, and punched number six on the panel. After a bit, Chad panted as he jogged the last few steps to where Patrick stood mischievously smiling with crossed arms.

"What took you so long, Dad?" he asked, belly laughing.

Chad drew him in for a hug as the two of them shared a special bonding moment before returning home. "I love you, son."

"I love you, too, Dad."

In the comfort of their Colorado home, Patrick cradled Tiff in his arms. Her bright, tiny eyes peered up at him. He spoke gently, telling her about his life—his best friend Curtis and their bubble gum pranks, Mr. Seitler's crazy classroom, the Hedge*witch* teacher who ruined fifth grade, losing Curtis and losing himself, and how he never remembered being anything but obese.

"I may still be heavy, but I'm more than my weight," he whispered. He went on to tell her about the old, dying man and his marbles; Mrs. Lee, Leigh, and Lissy; the yard sale, Mr. Jerry, and his mibsters; the draining practices; and the national tournament. "I've changed and I know who I am now," he said tickling her tummy. She squealed joyfully. "I love you, Tiffany Pickles! I'm your big brother, Patrick, Pudgy Knuckles!"

About the Author

Leah Lee was born and raised in the mountains of Colorado, and her favorite place to be is above timberline. She loves climbing mountains and has skied since the age of three. She still lives in a very small community with her husband, and they have five children.

She earned degrees in Law Enforcement, Criminal Justice, Psychology, and Elementary Education, as well as a Master's in Science Education. Leah taught for twelve years before having children. She homeschooled for eight years.

Leah spent twenty-seven years coaching the competitive game of marbles to Colorado youth and took many to the National Marbles Tournament.

Leah is the author of the *The Mark* and *Rockshire* series. She continues to write stories expressing her passionate faith in Jesus Christ.

www.ingramcontent.com/pod-product-compliance
Lightning Source LLC
Chambersburg PA
CBHW031558310726
48974CB00003B/723